NAGGING WIVES, FOOLISH HUSBANDS

FOOLISH HUSBANDS

THE SURREAL EXPERIENCES OF THE MARRIED LIFE

NAGGING WIVES, FOOLISH HUSBANDS

THE SURREAL EXPERIENCES OF THE MARRIED LIFE

a collection of short stories by

NATHANIEL TOWER

Nagging Wives, Foolish Husbands:
The Surreal Experiences of the Married Life
by Nathaniel Tower

First edition, February 2014. ISBN 978-0-615-97035-6.

Cover by Christopher Coffey. Book design by Julian Darius.

Stories in this collection have appeared in the following:
"A Happy Family" – *Bourbon Penn* Issue 1 (2011) and *Drabblecast* 220 (2011)
"Pregnancy and the Wildebeest, or, Laundry Day" – *The Old Timey Hedgehog* (2013)
"...And the Men Didn't Sleep" – *Rum Punch Press* (2013)
"Baby Steps" – *Foxing Quarterly* Issue 1 (2012)
"The Abortion Party" – *Drunk Monkeys* Anthology Volume One (2013)
"A Blade of Love" – *Bourbon Penn* Issue 3 (2012) and *Drabblecast* 233 (2012)
"Dead Man Sleeping" – *Liquid Imagination* Issue 7 (2010)
"The Arrival" – *This Zine Will Change Your Life* (2009)
"Living with a Giant Squid" – *Liquid Imagination* Issue 13 (2012)
"Quitting is Easy" – *Skive Magazine* Issue 13 (2009) and *(Short) Fiction Collective* (2011)
"Garbage Disposals, Wedding Rings and Potato Kings" – *Drunk Monkeys* (2012)
"Getting the Meat" – *Grim Corps* Issue 1 (2013)
"Skydivers and Pornographers" – *MuDJoB* (2012)
"Doctor Worthington's Lump" – *Drunk Monkeys* (2012)
"The Most Beautiful Toes" – *Marco Polo Arts* (2012)
"A Blade of Love, Part 2: Love's Sharp Blade" – *Gone Lawn* Issue 10 (2013)
"Steven Story and the Case of the Lost Balls" – *Martian Lit* (2012)
"The Ugly Husband" – *The Surreal Grotesque* Issue 1 (2012)
"The Flaming Skull" – *The Pedestal Magazine* 70 (2012)
"A Grand Unfurling" – *Untoward Magazine* (2011)
"Waiting for His Wife" – *SHINE!* (2008)

Published by Martian Lit. For more information about this or other titles, visit martianlit.com.

To my wife, for not being a nag, and for keeping me from being a fool.

Most of the time.

Contents

A Happy Family

After 36 hours of labor, my wife gave birth to a boot. It was brown leather. Size six. At first I was sure this meant she'd been unfaithful, but looking at her sweaty and poop covered body, I knew better than to question her.

So I asked the doctor privately if we could do a paternity test. He made the mistake of announcing the results in front of my wife. Sure enough, the boot was mine.

"Congratulations," the doctor said.

"Why didn't you think it was yours?" my wife asked.

I told her that no one in my family had ever fathered a boot before.

"You can't be sure of that."

She was right. I couldn't be.

"You could be a little sympathetic, you know. I did just give birth to a boot."

She said it with that wet-dog post-labor look.

"C'mon, it's made of flexible leather. It's not like it had spurs," I retorted, instantly knowing my words were both a triumph and a mistake.

I quickly changed the subject by asking the doctor if the boot would grow. It was too small to fit either of us.

He said he didn't see why not.

We took the boot home the same day, buckling it carefully into the car seat even though it didn't fit properly. We waited on naming it. We had names picked out. Isabella for a girl and Noah for a boy. Both names were my wife's choice. I wanted Hansel or Gretel. She thought those were stupid names. Neither of her names seemed fitting for the boot. She said that it didn't look like an Isabella or a Noah. I said she just wanted to save those names for a more human looking baby.

"How did the doctor not know we were having a boot?" I asked as we set the boot into the crib.

My wife blamed me at first. "This is because you made me eat all that red meat."

"It's probably because of all those damn vegetables you ate. I'm surprised the kid wasn't a celery stalk."

"That would've been better than a boot," she muttered.

I felt a bit bad that she said that right in front of the boot. I shooed her out of the room to give the boot some rest. On the way out, I couldn't help but think that the custard walls clashed with its skin.

After a long talk in the other room, we decided to love the boot as we would any other child. Then I realized that we had forgotten to turn the baby monitor on. I rushed into the nursery to check on the boot. It was a little stiff when I arrived, but it seemed just as alive as it had been before.

As all new parents do, we proudly sent out photos of everything our little boot did.

Some people had the nerve to ask for their shower gifts back. I wanted to tell them to go to hell, but my wife said we couldn't just in case we didn't have a boot next time around. I told her I wanted another boot. After all, what the hell was the point of having one? You couldn't wear it, and you sure couldn't sell it. It was nothing more than a decoration.

"We could fill it with soil and put a flower in it," I told her one day while we were changing the boot.

"It's our child you're talking about."

I could tell she meant business, but I figured she would be closer to it since she had carried it in her belly for nine months.

For the next few weeks it was nice because the boot was so quiet. It barely made a noise and required almost no changing at all. We found our lives a lot more manageable than all our friends and relatives had warned us it would be. But then we started to think that maybe all that silence wasn't good, that our boot wasn't developing like a normal baby should. We called the doctor, but he didn't really know what to say. He seemed surprised that we had kept the thing. Were we supposed to put it up for adoption?

We decided that the boot would be better off if we picked a gender and gave it a name. Eventually we called it Sam because we weren't quite sure if it was a boy or a girl. We thought it would be best if the boot decided when it got older.

After a year, the boot still wasn't talking or walking, and it wasn't eating very much. It didn't respond to Sam, so we tried Noah, Isabella, and Hansel, but it didn't seem to like any of those names either.

"I think he's depressed," my wife said, convinced the boot was a boy.

"Well, what are we going to do? We can't very well take him to a therapist," I replied, conceding the gender of the boot.

"Maybe we should make a sibling for him," she said with a seductive smile.

That night, we tried our best to make a sibling for the boot. Not knowing much about making shoes, we just did what came naturally.

A month later, my wife showed me the positive pregnancy test. We went and showed it to the boot, but he just sat in his crib and stared. We figured he just didn't quite understand what we were driving at, but we went ahead with our plans.

All of the doctor's visits went well, and even though we were supposed to be hoping for a boot, I could tell that my wife secretly wanted a little girl she could call Isabella. I thought she was being selfish, that we needed to hope for the best for our firstborn, but I knew better than to say such things, especially after last time.

When the ninth month rolled around, my wife went into labor. We packed up the car with all the necessities, strapped our little boot into the car seat, and sped off to the hospital. The labor was much more strenuous this time around, and the doctor finally said that my wife needed a C-section. We had both been hoping for a natural childbirth, but the doctor insisted.

The next hour was quite intense, but the doctors successfully delivered our second born. My wife fainted when she saw it, but I beamed with pride. It was beautiful.

The boot finally seemed happy when we introduced it to its new baby brother, a healthy size six foot. I was happy too, until they ran away together.

Pregnancy and the Wildebeest, or, Laundry Day

When Alfred Tennington awoke early one Saturday morning to clean his pregnant wife's intimate wear, he discovered a wildebeest in their laundry room.

At the sight of the creature, the plastic laundry basket slipped from his hands and pounded on the tile floor. Fortunately for Alfred, the wildebeest, too engrossed in its work, didn't look up. Alfred couldn't quite tell what sort of laundry it was doing, but he was certain he saw an open bottle of fabric softener resting at its side. Careful not to attract any attention to himself, Alfred pushed the door gently closed.

Convinced he was dreaming, Alfred quickly returned to bed, wrapped his arm around Susan, and shut his eyes hoping he would soon wake up for real. The warmth of her body permeated his clothing and calmed his terrified skin.

"What are you doing back in bed?" Susan asked as soon as his cold fingers caressed her swollen belly.

"You mean I actually got up?" Alfred recoiled his arm and used the hand to rub the crust from his inner eyelids. He watched it fall like giant flakes of dust onto the navy blue sheets. The flakes told him he was not dreaming. They also told him he would soon be washing the sheets.

"Of course you got up. You went down to do the laundry, remember?" She rolled her body and glanced at him. "You're being such a big help this morning. I really appreciate it."

Alfred looked away, afraid to tell his wife the bad news.

"What's wrong?" she asked after kissing his cheek.

"Honey, I'm sorry. I tried, but the machine's in use," he said trying not to alarm her.

"What else are you washing right now? Whatever's in there needs to come out now because you need to wash my undies. I'm wearing my last clean pair."

"But you have dozens of pairs in your drawer," Alfred protested.

"I don't like any of those. They don't fit well anymore."

"But I bought some of those for you," he answered. He recalled a special trip he made to the store a few weeks ago to buy several packages of her favorite underwear. He'd even brought some of her favorite pairs along with him to verify the new ones were the exact same.

"You sure did," she snapped. "But I don't like any of those. They don't fit right."

Alfred looked in disbelief. "But some of them are identical to the ones you wanted me to wash."

"No they aren't. They're similar. They're not the same. They don't fit right. All of the underwear I like is dirty." She looked at him and pouted, pulling his hand down to her pregnant belly as a reminder.

Touching Susan's belly made Alfred not want to argue any further. Ever since the third month of pregnancy, Alfred found it almost impossible to reason with her. He wanted to meet her every need, but sometimes she just made it so hard, like the time she wanted three Big Macs with no pickles, lettuce, mayonnaise, tomatoes or beef patties. He tried to explain they wouldn't be Big Macs, that he would just be bringing home bread. They already had bread, but she insisted that was what she wanted. Of course, when he got home, she told him the order was all wrong and refused to eat anything.

"Fine, I'll see what I can do." He rose from the bed and tiptoed down the stairs, hoping he'd imagined the quarter-ton animal. He didn't in fact know for sure that it had been a wildebeest anyway. He'd never actually seen one before. As far as he knew it could've been a gnu—which coincidentally he'd also never seen before—or possibly some other African animal that had no business being in his laundry room.

The white basket filled with two weeks' worth of women's underwear still rested on the floor beside the laundry room door. If the wildebeest was still doing laundry, it hadn't bothered to disturb Alfred's load.

When he opened the laundry room door and peered inside, the wildebeest stood there with several wool sweaters hanging from its thick pointed horns.

Alfred pushed the door shut. He tried to think of things he could do to pass the time. It wasn't really important what he did as long as he didn't return to bed. Susan would sleep and wouldn't have a clue that Alfred wasn't doing the laundry. He didn't want to start a fight. Obviously he couldn't tell her about the wildebeest because she would just assume he was lying. He wasn't about to stress her out over something she needn't know about. If she came downstairs, he would show her the wildebeest and she would understand. Of course, this could backfire if she demanded that he remove the wildebeest at once.

Listening to the laundry machine gyrate, Alfred decided to wait it out. He could hear the wildebeest's breath through the closed door, his heart speeding up with each snort. It couldn't stay in there doing laundry all day. After all, how much clothing could a wildebeest have? Alfred would wait patiently until the wildebeest finished its laundry and left. Content with his plan, he went to the front door and looked outside for the paper. It hadn't arrived yet. Nor had the sun.

He walked to the kitchen and thought about making himself a nice breakfast. He could even whip up something for Susan as a peace offering for not doing her wash. After checking the pantry for pancake mix and finding none, he decided he wasn't really hungry anyway. He did feel a little thirsty though. After opening the fridge and taking a quick swig of orange juice, he went to the kitchen table and had a seat. He couldn't help but glance over at the laundry room door every few seconds. If Susan had seen his constant head turns she would have accused him of being paranoid.

After a few minutes, Alfred grew restless, his legs bouncing underneath the table. Perhaps he was just going a bit crazy at the early hour. Or maybe he was just being a coward. Either way he knew it was time to face his fears. Susan wouldn't stay in bed all day, and she would want to shower and put on some of those clean panties shortly after getting up.

Alfred rose from the chair and marched to the laundry room door. He pressed his ear against the wood and listened for the sounds of water dripping, machines whirring, or animals breathing. He heard nothing. The wildebeest must've left through the attached garage.

Slowly this time, he turned the knob and pulled open the door. The wildebeest's massive frame occupied almost the entire room. Even had Alfred the nerve to do his wife's laundry with the creature in there, he didn't think there was any space.

This time there was no mistaking that the wildebeest saw him. It looked him straight in the eyes, snorted, and whirled its head around like a windmill, the sweaters flailing through the air but somehow remaining hooked to the animal's head. For a brief moment he wondered why the beast owned so many sweaters before he saw its tail flick violently. It looked ready to attack.

Alfred slammed the door shut, immediately regretting his action. Leaning against the door, he listened for any rustling from upstairs. When he was sure the bang of the door hadn't disturbed his wife, he sighed and wondered what to do next.

Ordinarily, Alfred would've had no problem doing Susan's laundry. He didn't even mind doing it at such an early hour. He enjoyed doing things for his pregnant wife. It made him feel worthwhile, like he was contributing something. Unfortunately, there was simply no way he could accomplish this task at the moment.

He thought about walking back upstairs and telling her he had thrown the undies in the wash, but he didn't want to face her when she inevitably found out he hadn't. Imagining her reaction, he wondered if perhaps facing the wildebeest might be a little easier. Disappointing a pregnant wife seemed far riskier than confronting a large grass eater.

"I'll just go in there and face him," he boldly decided aloud. He would try being polite at first, and if that didn't work, then he would simply ask the wildebeest to leave. This was his house after all, and the wildebeest had no right to do laundry there, especially without permission and especially when his wife needed his help.

With his left hand he grabbed the basket and held it firmly against his waist. His right hand lunged forward and pulled the door open forcefully. Secretly he hoped to frighten the wildebeest, although he knew that could have some deadly ramifications.

The wildebeest was still there, the sweaters hanging exactly as they had before. The creature's black eyes glared straight at Alfred. The monstrous beast hadn't altered its position in the slightest.

"Excuse me," Alfred managed, not really sure what else to say. He wasn't even sure the wildebeest would understand English. He tried to step inside the small room, but he couldn't figure out how to get around the giant.

The wildebeest continued to stare. After a long pause, it scraped a hoof menacingly across the floor. A piece of tile cracked under the pressure.

Alfred froze, unsure whether or not the creature intended to charge. He tried to close the door, but his muscles didn't respond to his brain's request. Too frightened to move, Alfred now understood why deer just stared as cars prepared to hit them.

"Do you mind?" the wildebeest asked after a while.

Alfred couldn't respond.

"Do you *mind*?" it repeated in a baritone.

"Do-do-do you mind if I use the washing machine?" Alfred finally asked in his most polite tone. His voice came out several octaves higher than the wildebeest's, a fact that embarrassed Alfred more than a little.

"How's about I let you know when I'm finished?" the wildebeest replied.

Alfred shook his head. This was impossible. Since it was impossible, he saw no harm in being brave. "Look," he said, "this is *my* washing machine. If you don't mind, I need to do my laundry now, so please step aside." Alfred wasn't sure where he expected the animal to step, but he certainly wasn't going to let him step inside the kitchen.

"As a matter of fact, I *do* mind," the wildebeest said. "I'll let you know when my sweaters are dry. I'm not going to go outside with wet sweaters hanging from my horns. Besides, I might decide to wash another load. I'm almost out of clean socks. Now scram." Alfred tried to determine if the wildebeest was wearing socks, but it stepped forward and lowered its sharp horns before he could get a good look.

Alfred's muscles sprang into action and the door slammed shut inches from the wildebeest's nose. He sprinted up the stairs and tried to hop into the bed, but his wife stopped him.

"Not so fast," she said, her body surrounded by a fort of pillows. "It's time for you to go to the farmer's market."

My God, thought Alfred, really taking a good look at his wife for the first time in weeks. *She's as big as a walrus.*

"Did you remember to use the fabric softener?"

"I didn't get the laundry in," Alfred stammered.

"What the hell do you mean you didn't get the laundry in? What were you doing down there all that time?" She wrestled her body into an upright position, the fort of pillows crashing down around her. He knew she had the right to complain. The woman was so big it seemed physical impossible for her to move.

"There's a wildebeest in the laundry room," he tried to reason with her.

"Yeah, well, there's a wildebeest in my stomach right now too." She glared at him sharply with her dark eyes.

Alfred didn't disagree. He just marched back downstairs, silently praying the wildebeest's sweaters were dry. All the while he couldn't help but wonder if maybe the wildebeest actually did belong in the laundry room after all.

Suddenly fueled by chivalry Alfred pulled the door open, stomped his foot, and wagged a finger at the stunned wildebeest. "Look, buddy," he shouted right in the creature's ear, "I've got some laundry to do. It's important. You need to get out. If you have something you really need washed, I'll put it in for you. But I can't have you just standing around taking up all this room."

The wildebeest let out a little snort before flinging a sweater off an antler. He pawed it to make sure it was dry.

"I'm almost done," the wildebeest said. "But don't push your luck. I'm a guest after all. You should show me some respect."

"Respect my ass," Alfred said, refusing to back down now. "You're trespassing. You don't belong here."

"Don't I?" the wildebeest asked.

"No, you don't. You're not wanted here. And you take up too much space. Now move so I can do my wife's laundry."

The wildebeest's sharp eyes made Alfred quiver. The beast let out an angry snort, steam rising from its nostrils.

"Look, buddy, I don't need this. I have every right to be here. But I'll tell you what, since I'm such a nice guy. You leave the basket here and I promise I'll get the underwear into the wash."

Alfred nodded his head and said, "That sounds reasonable." He evaluated the wildebeest's demeanor, trying to determine if the thing was really trustworthy.

The wildebeest, somehow sensing Alfred's skepticism, responded, "Hey, I know you don't believe me. But you can trust me," it said while holding up a hoof.

"And how do I know that?" Alfred asked.

"Let's just say I'm invested in all this." The wildebeest felt the other sweaters. Satisfied with their dryness, he folded them into a nice stack.

At the wildebeest's suggestion, Alfred lashed out, swinging his fists in the monster's direction.

"What are you doing?" the wildebeest asked, seemingly unfazed by the blows of Alfred's clenched fists.

"Get out of my house!" Alfred shouted.

The wildebeest pushed Alfred away gently. Grabbing the sweaters, the wildebeest said, "I don't have to take this abuse. I can do my laundry elsewhere." Before the wildebeest turned to leave through the garage attached to the laundry room, it scooped up Susan's panties and marched out the door without another word.

"Hey, what the hell?" Alfred yelled.

The wildebeest looked back at Alfred but didn't say a word before leaving with its sweaters and Susan's underwear.

Defeated, Alfred slowly walked up the stairs, his head hanging low in embarrassment as he prepared to deliver the bad news to his wife. On the way up the stairs, he wondered how he could be a father when he couldn't even defend his wife's sacred panties against an oversized deer. This wasn't the first time he'd doubted himself as a father, but the other doubts were all the insignificant and normal fears of any father-to-be. He was sure those would all go away the moment he held that new crying child for the first time.

At the top of the stairs, Alfred looked in at his slumbering wife. He admired the way she breathed slowly and audibly, somehow fighting off the discomfort brought by the beast inside her. Seeing her made him want to find the wildebeest and take him out. But he knew better. There was no sense in chasing wildebeests around town when he had other things to do. Without entering the room, he blew her a kiss and turned back down the stairs. He grabbed his keys and headed for the farmer's market, hoping that one of those stands with the pretty handmade jewelry would be open. She deserved something nice for all her work. As he drove, he vowed he wouldn't disappoint her again.

At the farmer's market, Alfred picked out the delicious fresh fruits and vegetables his wife craved so much. From ripe avocados to fragrant cantaloupe, he filled his canvas bags with everything he could hold. With his arms nearly bursting under the weight of the food, he walked around until he found a homemade jewelry stand with gorgeous accent pendants. He set his produce down and fingered a beautiful necklace. He was about to say, "I'll take this one," when he spotted the wildebeest set up behind a little wooden stand.

Alfred released the necklace. Without picking up his food, he walked over to the wildebeest. He cleared his throat

"And what are you selling today?" Alfred asked.

"Some underwear," the wildebeest said.

"How much?" Alfred asked, knowing he'd pay any price to get Susan's possessions back. As much as he was appalled at the fact that the wildebeest was selling used, *dirty* laundry that wasn't even his, Alfred could think of nothing but satisfying his wife at the moment. Usually he scoffed skeptically at almost every purchase. "We don't need that," he constantly told Susan. Now he knew better.

"Ten bucks a pair," the wildebeest said.

"I'll take them all," Alfred said.

The wildebeest piled Susan's panties into the bag while Alfred pulled out his wallet. He wondered if the wildebeest recognized him. Surely he did.

The wildebeest handed the bag over before Alfred handed him the money. "We'll call it even at a hundred," the wildebeest said, as if cutting Alfred a deal.

He knew now was the time to be bold.

"I think we're already even," Alfred said as he turned and ran, grabbing the bags of produce he'd left on the ground on his way to the car.

He looked back in terror only once. The wildebeest wasn't chasing him. It wasn't even calling attention to the theft. Alfred had won after all.

As soon as he got home, Alfred locked the door and tossed the underwear in the wash, not bothering to clean off the wildebeest fur that covered the machine.

While the machine whirred away, Alfred put the produce away, then went upstairs and sat in the rocking chair in the baby's room. He looked at all the furniture he still had to assemble. For the first time ever, Alfred felt ready.

Gorilla Guest

When Mark and Janie Penteller moved into their dream home—complete with foyer, crown molding, *and* vaulted ceilings—they expected all of their dreams would come true; they certainly didn't expect to find a quarter-ton Eastern Lowland Gorilla sitting on the bed in the guestroom. It was the only thing out of place in the new house, but it didn't make up for the lack of the widow's walk that Janie had desperately wanted. Mark promised he would build her one someday, the final piece that finally encouraged Janie to agree to buy.

Not minding for the moment that there was no widow's walk, Janie and Mark walked hand-in-hand through each room of the house, admiring their high ceilings and soft carpets. Until they found the gorilla, sitting on the bed with its back to the door.

Mark dialed the realtor right away—after Janie slammed the door shut, of course.

"Are you all settled in already?" the realtor asked, as if she cared. The only thing she cared about was the fat stack of cash sitting in her pocket after the half-million dollar transaction.

"There's a gorilla in the guest bedroom," Mark said.

"Where's it supposed to go?" the realtor asked.

"It's not supposed to be here at all."

"Were the movers supposed to leave it behind?"

"No. We've never had a gorilla. It shouldn't be there at all."

"Are you sure it's a gorilla?"

"Yes, I'm sure. The thing is seven feet tall. I didn't just conjure it up in my mind."

"I think you're exaggerating," the realtor said. "Gorillas only get to be about six feet tall."

"Who the hell are you? Jane Goodall?"

Janie interrupted from the stairs. "Jane Goodall worked with chimps, not gorillas."

Mark covered the phone with his hand. "What the hell does it matter what she worked with?"

"If you're going to make a reference, you should at least get it right."

"Whatever. She worked with monkeys. What difference does it make?" Mark removed his hand and started to speak into the phone, but the realtor interrupted.

"She's right, you know," the realtor said. "And they aren't monkeys. They're apes."

"Okay, I'm not going to debate this. What are we going to do about the gorilla in our house?"

"Call the movers. I'm sure it was all a mistake. They'll take care of it. Enjoy the new house." The realtor hung up before Mark could get in another word.

"Well, that was sure helpful."

"What do you expect?" Janie said. "She already got the money out of us. Taking care of a gorilla isn't in her job description."

"I doubt it's in the mover's job description either," Mark said. He searched through an envelope for the moving receipt. Finding it, he dialed the number.

"Enjoying the new house?" the woman on the other end said after Mark introduced himself.

"No, actually. You left a gorilla in here. An Eastern Lowland Gorilla."

"Sir," the woman began, "I can assure you that our movers take great care with all of your possessions. Customer service is our number one priority. If you aren't satisfied, we will take care of it."

"Okay. So come and get the gorilla."

"We'll send your movers over right away," the woman said.

"Great. Thank you." He hung up and told his wife the good news.

"And you didn't think they would take care of it," Janie said.

The two began unpacking boxes in the kitchen while they waited for the movers to arrive. Neither wanted to venture upstairs. They were glad the gorilla at least knew his place in the house. As unwelcome as he was, he was still a guest.

The movers arrived within the hour, the same three movers who had loaded and unloaded all of their furniture and boxes the day before.

"What's the problem?" the straw-haired one asked.

"You left a gorilla in here by mistake," Mark said.

"Not possible," the shortest mover said. His stocky legs burst through ripped jean shorts, revealing intricately designed tattoos with no seeming symbolic significance. Probably the work of a drunken mind.

"Well, it's up there. And it wasn't up there when we did the final walk through." Mark pointed to the ceiling.

"Show us," the short one said.

Mark led them up the curved staircase. "He's in the guest room," Mark said as they tramped up the plush stairs. "But he's certainly not *our* guest."

The movers followed without a word, but Mark could feel their scoffing judgment on his back.

When Mark pushed open the guestroom door, the movers collectively inhaled.

"That's a damn gorilla," the short one said.

"Yeah, it sure is," Straw said.

"Told ya so," Mark said.

The four men stared at the beast, its back still facing them. In awe, they watched its shoulders heave up and down, rippling muscles making a waterfall in its back.

"So what are you going to do about it?" Mark said after they had all soaked in the sight.

"That's not our problem," Shorty said. "We didn't put that here."

"Well I sure didn't."

"Like I said, not our problem." He signaled to the others and they headed down the stairs, not waiting for Mark to lead the way.

"You can't just leave him there," Mark hollered after them.

"We can't take him. We don't move living things. We thought you wanted us to remove a statue."

"Who the hell has a seven-foot gorilla statue?" Mark shouted as they headed out the door.

"I don't know. But there's no way that thing was seven feet tall."

Mark wasn't about to have this conversation again.

The three movers headed to the truck.

"Hey. Get back in there and take him out."

The movers didn't respond.

"I'm going to write a bad review," Mark said.

"Of course," the silent-until-now mover said. "Be sure to mention that we left a live gorilla by accident. I'm sure that will give your review a lot of credibility."

Mark was so surprised by the mover's strong vocabulary and quick wit that he was left nonplussed while the moving truck started and sped away.

"Stupid movers," Mark said when he went back in the house.

Janie shook her head. "I want that gorilla out of my house."

"I'll take care of it."

"Good. You better. I'm going to the grocery store for some food. I guess I better get a shitload of bananas."

Janie left without offering a kiss to Mark. The magic the house was supposed to bring them was turning out to be the black kind.

Frustrated, Mark plopped on the couch and tried to concoct a plan to remove the beast. After a few minutes, he slouched back and closed his eyes, hoping the answer would come in his slumber.

When Janie returned home from the grocery store and asked if the gorilla was still there, Mark opened his eyes and shrugged. He didn't bother getting off the couch.

"I told you to take care of that," she said.

"And I said that I would."

"Well, do it already."

"These things take time," Mark said. "You can't reason with it. I need to develop a thorough plan."

"Well, don't develop too much. You better get started on that widow's walk, while you're at it. If you don't get rid of that gorilla soon, we're going to need it."

Mark shook his head. He wanted to explain that this made no sense. He had no need for a widow's walk, and if she did follow through on this implied threat, it wouldn't matter to him if she had a place to walk or not.

"Don't be such a nag," he said. "I'll take care of it."

"I wouldn't have to be such a nag if you weren't such a fool," Janie said before storming off to the basement.

Mark sighed and walked upstairs. He hated being called a fool, and he wasn't going to let an unwanted gorilla make him look like one. Without knocking, he shoved the door open and yelled to the gorilla, "Okay, buddy, time to leave."

The gorilla didn't move. Its heaving breaths ceased, and in the silence, Mark thought he heard a sniffle from the gargantuan figure's nostrils.

"Are you okay?" he asked.

The gorilla turned. Tears pooled around its yellow eyes.

"What's wrong?"

The gorilla didn't say a word, reaching a silent finger up and wiping the moisture away.

Mark searched his pockets for a tissue, but all he found was a dime and a paperclip. He approached the gorilla and sat down on the bed beside it. The gorilla didn't look so big anymore. Certainly not seven feet tall.

"What's the problem?" Mark asked again.

The gorilla still said nothing, which Mark had come to expect by now. It was one thing for a gorilla to inexplicably show up in his house. It was another thing entirely for that gorilla to communicate in a civilized manner.

Mark slid his arm around the ape. Its sharp and wiry hair poked Mark's delicate skin, and he almost recoiled his consolation offering. Before he could react, the gorilla leaned into Mark's shoulder, accepting the gesture of compassion.

"Can I get you something to eat?" Mark asked, not knowing what else to say to comfort the still-sniffling primate. He'd never done well when it came to dealing with sad people, and dealing with sad apes was no different. Whenever Janie cried, Mark would hold her for a while, but there was never anything much else he could figure to do, other than ask if there was anything he could do. The answer, of course, was always no.

The ape's head bobbed, which Mark interpreted as yes. He removed his arm and jogged down to the kitchen. He rushed to make a peanut butter and banana sandwich, the only thing he could think to make for such a creature. There was only one piece of whole wheat bread left, so he made the sandwich on sourdough. He hoped the ape wouldn't mind.

Along with the sandwich, he brought a glass of milk and several bottles of condiments—relish, yellow mustard, spicy brown mustard, honey mustard, and mayonnaise. He really wasn't sure what gorillas wanted on their sandwiches.

The gorilla was still in the same spot on the bed. Mark handed him the plate and asked him what he wanted on the sandwich. The gorilla picked up the sandwich, stared at the bread, then chucked the thing against the window.

"Hey!" Mark yelled. "I put a lot of effort into that. It has bananas on it!"

The ape made no response.

"Aren't you hungry?"

Mark thought the ape's head swayed side to side.

"How can you not be hungry? You must be starving!"

The ape grunted.

Mark looked into the creature's black and yellow eyes. It felt like the time when he was a kid and stared into a well trying to see the water. He couldn't see the water then, and he couldn't see anything inside the gorilla now. He took this as deep hurt and depression.

Mark breathed in deeply, trying to figure out what to do. The gorilla's repulsive odor entered his nostrils.

"Let's get you outside for a bath," Mark said. If he had to have this giant thing in his house, he was at least going to make sure it didn't stink up the place.

Mark stood and offered a hand to the gorilla. "Come on, let's go."

The gorilla reached out its hand and started to rise, its force pulling Mark into its lap. The gorilla plopped down on the bed, Mark's face now buried in its hairy crotch.

As luck would have it, Janie entered the room at the precise moment Mark found himself entangled in the beast's pubic hair, if it was called pubic hair on a gorilla.

"What the heck is going on here?" Janie roared, her arms thrown in frustration. "I leave for an hour and you're hooking up with a gorilla!"

"It's not what it looks like," Mark said, his face still pressed against the gorilla.

"Then what is it?"

"I thought he was hungry." The gender of the beast was no surprise to Mark anymore. "I brought him a sandwich."

Mark pulled his head out of the crotch and looked at Janie. She laughed.

"What's so funny?"

"There's gorilla fur on your face."

I laughed too and wiped my face.

"I think it's stuck in my teeth." Mark spit a couple times.

"Let me help." Janie approached Mark and started brushing the hair off his face. They giggled and he sat down and pulled her onto his lap.

The gorilla stood up and walked out of the room.

"Where are you going?" Mark called to him. The gorilla didn't respond.

"Should we follow him?" Janie asked.

"Yeah, we better. We don't want him to terrorize the house."

The couple exchanged a quick kiss then followed the gorilla downstairs without a word. They stalked after him into the kitchen and watched as he raided the newly-filled pantry.

The gorilla tossed boxes and bottles to the floor. A glass jar shattered on the hardwood.

"Should we stop him?" Janie asked.

"I don't know. He looks pretty angry."

The gorilla continued flinging boxed food out of the pantry until the shelves were as barren as when the Pentellers had moved in just a few hours before. Unsatisfied, the beast stomped to the refrigerator and pulled it open, tugging the door clean off in the process. Mark was uncertain where the sudden aggression came from, but he thought it somehow had to do with hunger and Janie's presence.

"Do something," Janie pleaded to Mark.

Mark approached the gorilla. "Hey buddy, can I help you find something?"

The gorilla swung a hairy fist at the air surrounding Mark, then pulled more food out of the refrigerator. When he discovered the bag of spinach in the crisper, he tore it open and emptied the contents into his mouth at once. He tossed the bag on the floor then spit the dry green leaves back into the refrigerator.

"Hey," Mark yelled, for some reason expecting the single syllable to deter the creature's violent raid.

The gorilla continued spitting spinach into the fridge until his mouth must have been empty. Then he galloped for the backdoor, knocking over everything in his way. Without waiting for their assistance, the ape jumped through the glass. Mark and Janie watched in silent awe as the hairy beast leapt off their two-story deck and trotted into the woods, his unscathed body powering through the thick brush.

Mark and Janie walked over to the door and watched until they couldn't see any remnants of the ape.

"Do you think he'll be back?" Janie asked.

Mark shrugged. "I don't know, but we better not buy any more spinach just in case."

They hugged each other. In their make-up embrace, they looked out the broken glass for any sign of reason.

"Why do you think he was here?" Janie asked.

"I don't know, but it feels really nice outside. Want to go on a picnic?"

Janie accepted Mark's request and the couple dined on a blanket in the backyard, their heads turning to the woods every few minutes for any sign of the gorilla.

"I think he's gone for good," Mark said as they packed up the blanket and trash.

"Well, let's hope so."

They stood in the yard, their picnic all wrapped up. "It's a nice house," Janie said.

"Yeah, yeah it is," Mark said.

"Shall we go back inside?"

"I don't know. It's kind of nice out here. It's good enough for the gorilla. Maybe he was just trapped. Maybe he just wanted out."

Mark put his arm around Janie. She looked into the woods.

"Do you want to try to find him? See what his life is like?"

Mark smiled. "Let's do it."

They dropped their picnic supplies to the ground and ran off into the woods, their arms pounding against the grass as they imitated the mighty gorilla's run.

...And the Men Didn't Sleep

There was a village in which the men didn't sleep. They hadn't slept since the first baby had been born many years ago. The babies, as well as their wives, wouldn't let them sleep.

The noise was constant. Worse than the buzzing of machines. The women had somehow blocked it out, but the men lay sleepless all night. They had tried earplugs, but those hadn't worked for more than a few minutes. The babies figured out the men couldn't hear them so they learned to scream louder.

One day, Adam, who'd grown tired of being tired, built a machine. Adam built a device to solve all of the men's problems—and hopefully cause a few problems for the women.

The device silenced all of the babies. It de-cried them. No matter how hungry or how tired or how lonely a baby was, he or she just couldn't cry. And Adam became a hero.

Soon men were sleeping all night and well into the morning. Some men slept for days or weeks at a time. One man reportedly slept for a month.

The women, on the other hand, stayed up all the time begging their children to cry so they would know when they were hungry or tired or in need of changing or coddling. But the children didn't cry, and the mothers tried coddling them when they were hungry and feeding them when they were tired and putting them down to sleep when they wanted to be coddled.

The women were far too tired and too busy trying to figure out what was wrong with their children. The food went uncooked and the homes and clothes went uncleaned. This didn't bother the men much because they were sleeping all the time anyway. No matter how much the women nagged and complained, the men just rolled over and went to sleep, as if they were sleeping off decades of tiredness.

Finally, a woman called Ava grew tired of being so tired and having a husband who slept so much. Ava decided to build a machine of her own. Her machine was much simpler in design than Adam's machine, but it did so much more. Whereas Adam's machine left babies unable to cry, Ava's machine left men unable to experience pleasure. Coincidentally, the only thing the men did besides sleep these days was engage in pleasures of the flesh. But not after Ava's machine was finished.

Once the women all knew the effects of Ava's machine, their libidos became insatiable. They made their husbands please them seven, eight, ten times a day and then ordered the men to take care of the babies as a thank you for their tireless efforts in bed. The men did as they were told because there wasn't really anything else for them to do anyway.

The children still wouldn't cry and the men couldn't figure out what to do with them, but the women were so exhausted from the sex that they didn't care much. The men were tired as well because they had stopped sleeping to care for the babies and for want of pleasure they just couldn't achieve.

One night, Adam set out to break Ava's machine. On the same night, Ava set out to break Adam's machine. Babies started to cry and men started to howl in delight. There was so much crying and so much sex over the next ten hours that soon everyone in the whole village was just so tired that they all went down for a nap that lasted weeks. And when they woke up, everything seemed at peace.

Baby Steps

When our baby started crawling at three weeks, my wife and I asked the doctor if it was normal even though we knew it wasn't.

"There's no cause for alarm," he told us. "Developmental milestones come at all different ages."

I asked if he'd ever heard of a baby crawling at three weeks. He told me he hadn't, but then he added that he'd never heard of anything before it happened for the first time. I guess that was supposed to be reassuring, but when we got home and Sophie stepped right out of her car seat, I knew things were moving too fast. Shelly agreed and said we needed to do something.

Sophie walked around the living room—without bumping into anything or even stumbling the slightest—while I called the doctor to tell him the latest news. He sounded unimpressed, like I was just wasting his time.

"You have to let kids develop according to their own schedule," he told me.

Even though I didn't fully trust the doctor, I took his advice. He had been a pediatrician for twenty years, after all, and watching Sophie stomp around the house like she owned the place was certainly better than listening to her scream like a banshee the way our friends' babies did.

But that was only the start of our troubles.

Within a week, Sophie wasn't just walking around and talking; she was giving us orders. Twice she commandeered my medium-rare steak and made me drink her watery formula instead. She made me wash all of her outfits three times before she would wear them, and my wife had to return half the clothes she had bought because "the buttons weren't cute enough."

Of course we acquiesced to her every request. She was just a baby, and all the books told us to provide for her every need. None of them quite prepared us for all these needs though.

By the time she hit that big one month mark, she was sleeping in our king size bed. And I don't mean with us. I was sleeping on the couch and Shelly was sleeping on the air mattress. Don't think she got the better deal either. The air mattress deflated within an hour every night, and when we tried to pump it back up on the second night of our exile, Sophie stormed downstairs and told us to quit making so much racket. She threatened to give us nothing but formula and mashed squash for the next month. We silently slipped back into our respective sleeping quarters, sans sheets, both of us cowering and shaking until sleep finally came over us just minutes before Sophie announced she needed some deviled eggs. She threw out the first two batches before she was finally satisfied with the product.

We apologized fervently for all of our parenting errors, but she refused to accept and confiscated our phones and car keys.

I can't even say how much humiliation I felt that morning when my daughter, not even five weeks old, dropped me off at work. To make matters even worse, she told me to take the bus home because she had "some errands to run." What type of errands a five-week old could possibly do was beyond me. Would anyone even take her seriously if she tried to make a purchase?

I'd never ridden a bus before in my life. The system seemed so complex; I ended up boarding four different buses before I somehow managed to find myself a few blocks from our house.

Unfortunately, when I got home, Shelly was sitting on the porch with one small suitcase.

"It's for both of us," she said before showing me the eviction noticed signed by Sophie.

"At least we have our credit cards and bank accounts," I said as we marched to the nearest motel.

Of course I spoke too soon.

"Your card was declined," the clerk—or whatever the hell she's called—at the cheap motel informed me when we tried to check in.

"Run this one," I told her.

"Also declined," she said unenthusiastically after a quick swipe. The way she eyed us I could tell she thought we were just there for a quickie before we had to go back home to our spouses.

"Do you have any cash?" I asked Shelly, not wanting to explain our situation to this over eye-shadowed motel worker.

"I spent all mine in the vending machine because Sophie wouldn't let me pack a lunch," she replied. "What about you?"

"I spent all mine on the bus ride home," I responded

We pleaded with the woman to just let us stay for the night. We swore we were good for it.

"Hotel policy," she said as she snapped her gum and looked for something to distract herself from our sob story.

"Then I need to see the manager," I demanded.

The manager, a puny just-post teenager, wouldn't budge either. When he showed us the door, I thought he was going to give us parenting advice. Like we needed advice on how to raise our kid from a motel manager.

With nowhere else to turn, we called our doctor. We had to make a collect call from what may very well have been the world's last working payphone tucked behind a 7-Eleven. I wished I could've gotten a Wild Cherry Slurpee while I was there.

Luckily, our doctor accepted the charges for the call. What a saint.

"She's taking over everything," I said. "And it's all your fault," I added for good measure.

"It's hardly my fault," he responded. "She's your kid. You need to learn to control her."

"But you said to let her make her own schedule," I reminded him.

"Sure, but I didn't say to let her take over the world."

"Well, you owe us. At least give us a place to stay for the night," I begged.

He thought about it for a while before offering us one of the patient rooms at his office. He made it very clear that it was for one night only, and he told us we had to stay in the room with the creepy skeleton and the weird paper dolls.

I didn't bother to say thank you.

"Oh, and one more thing," he added. "I'm adding this phone call to your next bill."

I told Shelly that we needed a new pediatrician after I hung up.

She was just relieved that we had a place to stay for the night.

"Should we at least call Sophie and tell her where we are?" my wife wondered as we got ready for bed in room 3.

"Oh yeah, I'm sure she's really concerned about that," I spat through a mouthful of toothpaste that I was fortunate enough to brush with a three-year old toothbrush that had previously been demoted to cleaning the grout in our shower.

"She is only five weeks old," she replied as she removed her makeup with an alcohol wipe she found in one of the drawers.

"It sure doesn't seem like it," I said after spitting into the tiny sink. "I know I didn't act like that when I was five weeks old."

"You don't remember that far back." I glanced at her and thought for a moment that the alcohol wipe had peeled away some of the flesh from her cheeks. I decided not to mention it.

She was right. I didn't remember, but I figured my parents would've just smacked me once and my reign of terror would've been over.

We didn't say another word as we climbed onto the patient table. It was a tight squeeze, reminding me of the old college dorm days when we tried to share the twin bed. This was a lot less comfortable.

In the morning, we decided to drive by the house just to see if Sophie was doing okay on her own.

She was holding a container of formula powder and crying on the tire swing in the front yard when we got there.

Shelly began crying too and ran to comfort her.

"Where have you been?" Sophie demanded. "I've been worried sick about you. How could you just abandon me like that?"

Of course Shelly burst into apologetic sobs, as if it had been her fault. But I took a different approach.

"Sophie, your mother and I are putting our foot down right now. We're the boss, not you. From now on, you will do what we say or you won't do anything at all."

Her bottom lip quivered as the tear droplets swelled in her eyes.

"Don't give me that look," I demanded before telling her she was grounded.

"You can't ground me," she shouted back. "I'm leaving this house forever." She sprinted to the car and drove away before I could stop her.

I found her four weeks later working as a waitress in a rundown pub. She looked miserable when she took my drink order. "Can I come home, Daddy?" she begged.

"Sorry, I don't take strangers home," I told her before telling her to bring my beer in a frosty mug.

Watching her little body waddle away, I couldn't help but feel the whole thing had been my fault. I wondered how I could have been a better dad. Did I not read enough books during the pregnancy? Did I not hold her long enough the first time she cried? Somewhere, I must've done something wrong.

When she placed my beer in a frosty mug down on the table, I stood, picked her up high, and carried her out to the car. She didn't even protest when I strapped her into the baby seat in the back.

That night Shelly and I had sex for the first time in six months.

When we were finished, we both whispered a silent prayer that another one wouldn't be on the way. At least that's what my prayer was.

But before I could fall asleep, I found myself hovering over Sophie's crib, watching her steady breathing. The way her chubby little stomach rose up and down was just adorable. Without waking up, she let loose a little smile. I knew that I would give her whatever she wanted in the morning.

The Abortion Party

Jared had to look at the invitation three times before he understood what it said. Even then, he wasn't quite sure he believed it. He brought it to his wife Deborah and asked what she thought.

"What the hell is a 'Pregnancy Termination party'?" he asked her.

"Oh, did we get Sherry's invite today?" Deborah responded, reaching out in anticipation.

"Is this like an abortion shower or something?"

"Sounds a little crude when you put it that way," she said. "It's just a way of celebrating the reversal of an accident. Not everyone wants a kid, you know."

"You aren't seriously planning on attending this, are you?"

"Of course. She's my friend."

"What do you bring for a gift? A bent coat hanger?"

Deborah gave an icy stare. "She's not a barbarian. It's not like this is some back alley procedure. This is a growing trend. If people can celebrate being pregnant, why can't they celebrate not being pregnant?"

"So do you bring a gift?" Jared asked.

"Of course. It is a party. She's registered at Bed, Bath and Beyond."

Jared glanced at the invitation again. "Do they have a specific registry for this kind of thing?"

"Don't be so dense. You can register for anything. Besides, you're being rude. She just wants to celebrate with her friends."

He looked up from the postcard. "Do I have to go?"

"Your name's on the invitation, isn't it?"

"So is this a couple's shower?"

"Well, they're both not having a baby, right?"

Jared shook his head and tossed the invitation on the table. "I'm opposed to the whole idea."

"It's her body," Deborah defended her friend.

"That's not what I mean." Jared threw his hands up. "You know I'm a fairly open-minded guy. But we're talking about celebrating *nothing*. We're not having a baby either right now, and you don't see us having a party for it. This is just a cheap ploy for gifts."

"But we didn't have to go through anything to not have the baby we're not having. They went through a lot. We can at least show our support. I think we should get the crystal set." Deborah pulled up the couple's registry on her iPhone and waved it in Jared's face. He stepped back to see the tiny screen.

"$75! You've got to be kidding."

Deborah pulled back the phone and glanced at the small picture. "Do you think that's too cheap? You know that's per piece, right. Should we get something else as well?"

"Too cheap! I would think a $10 paper towel holder would be sufficient." He grabbed the phone from her hand and scrolled through the registry. "This is insane. Everything on here is over $50. And what do they need all this junk for? Place settings for 12? It's not like they're adding anyone to the family."

She grabbed the phone back. "I'm ordering the crystal. I'm supporting my friend. And you're going to the party and you're going to put on a good face and be nice to everybody."

"Whatever," he said before retreating to his home office to check his email and research pregnancy termination parties. After a few minutes, he gave up his search and opted for some lesbian porn. If these pregnancy termination parties really were popular, they were secretly popular. Not like lesbian porn. That was widely popular, which pleased Jared immensely.

The party wasn't mentioned again until Deborah came downstairs one Saturday with a dress on.

"Where are you going in that?" Jared asked.

"What do you mean? We've got Sherry's party to go to today. It starts in an hour. Why the hell're you wearing that stupid cut-off t-shirt?"

Jared thought Deborah looked sexy in the dress, although he hadn't noticed this until she'd started nagging him. He didn't bother to tell her though. Deborah didn't seem to like it much when he told her she was sexy. Instead, he turned off the TV and went upstairs to put on what Deborah would consider "proper public attire."

"Is this okay?" he asked when he came down a few minutes later, wearing the nice jeans and orange polo she had picked out for him about a week ago, saying as she handed it to him, "This would look great at a party." He figured that was some sort of hint.

"No. That's not okay," Deborah said before she even looked at Jared. "You look like a bum. We're going to a special occasion, not a frat party."

Jared looked down and shrugged. He thought he looked pretty good, even if he had been skeptical of the outfit when she had first presented it to him. "Okay. I'll change. What do you want me to wear?"

"You're not a child," Deborah said. "You can pick out your own outfit. Just pick out something that isn't embarrassing."

Jared went back upstairs, his mind already made up what he would wear. He'd wear the same khakis and blue striped shirt he always wear when they went anywhere. The good thing was they so seldom went anywhere that it was likely no one had seen him in the outfit, or at least no one would remember seeing him with it on.

When he came back down a few minutes later, Deborah said, still not looking, "Do you have to wear that *again*? You wore that last time we saw Sherry?"

Jared put up a fight this time. "I haven't seen Sherry since before she got pregnant. There's no way in hell she would remember what I was wearing. And if she did, then she's superficial and I don't care what she thinks anyway."

"Does that mean I'm superficial and you don't care what I think?"

"Of course not. It's your job to make sure I look okay. You need to notice what I'm wearing. But Sherry doesn't have any business criticizing my wardrobe. Especially not in her condition."

"And just what is *that* supposed to mean?" The hands were suddenly on the hips, and Jared felt sweat droplets slide down from his armpits.

"I'll go change," he said, one more outfit on his mind.

When he returned a few minutes later in the same khakis and the orange polo he'd tried before, Deborah told him it was time to go. She didn't bother to say anything about how he looked, and he wasn't sure if she noticed that all he'd done was mixed the two outfits. He wondered if he could've come down in a clown suit with a giant dildo growing out of his forehead. Maybe she had a two nag limit on clothing choices. Whatever the case, Jared was just glad they were getting on their way, although he was still pissed off about the whole thing. But that was okay with him because he had a plan. Hiding his devious smile, he hopped into the car and headed for Sherry's party with his silent wife seated next to him, a stack of perfectly wrapped presents in her lap.

"How many presents did you get her?" he asked after they'd traveled a few miles.

"You mean 'we,'" she replied.

"Okay, fine. How many presents did *we* get her?"

"They aren't just for her, you know. They're for her husband too."

"Of course they are. I forgot they *both* weren't having this baby."

He waited for her to tell him what gifts they were bringing. After three blocks of silence, he spoke again.

"So I'm still unsure of this whole thing. Do they actually perform the abortion there?"

"No. Don't be an ignorant ass. Of course they don't. They aren't barbarians. This isn't some sort of animalistic ritual sacrifice to some crop gods. Sherry went to the doctor yesterday. It should be taken care of."

"How do you know? Have you ever been to one of these before?" He glanced at her, but she didn't return his glance.

"No. I've never been to one. I'm just sure they don't do it at the party. That's a private thing, after all. Have you ever been to a baby shower where the baby is birthed?"

Jared shook his head. "I don't get why we're celebrating. I'm not opposed to a woman's right to choose, but I don't see why anyone would go around announcing this choice."

"It wasn't just her choice, you know," Deborah said while shifting the gifts in her lap. "They *both* made the decision. Sherry said it was more Adam's decision than hers. Some married couples actually make decisions together, you know."

Jared glanced at her quickly, but her eyes were still glued to the road, ready to correct his slightest driving error. "Of course. I know that. I also hear that some wives don't nag their husbands about every little thing."

"Yeah. I've heard that too. And I've also heard the one about the husband who wasn't a complete dumbass."

The snarky back-and-forth was making Jared a little horny, but he knew it wouldn't be right to proposition his wife for sex on the way to a party that celebrated the lack of procreation. Maybe the feeling would still be there when they got home that night. Or maybe he could just jerk off in the bathroom at Sherry's party. He snickered at the idea of getting semen on the toilet seat and

Sherry getting pregnant as a result. Even though it was just one of those silly urban legends, he couldn't help but laugh out loud at the thought.

"What the hell're you laughing at?" Deborah asked when Jared's snickering sent a stream of spit flying to the windshield.

"Nothing," Jared said. "Just thinking about some joke I heard at work."

"Well, keep it to yourself. I don't want you ruining the party with any stupid joke."

Jared laughed for a few more seconds, then the couple drove the rest of the way to the party in near silence. An occasional snort escaped Deborah's lips, usually followed by some type of chortle out of Jared's nose.

"Okay, we're here," Deborah said, announcing the obvious when Jared parked the car and turned off the engine. "Now remember to be nice. They've been through a lot."

"I thought they were celebrating."

"Well, yeah, but it's not like they won something."

"But I thought—"

"Never mind what you thought. Let's just get inside and get this party started." Her voice rose in excitement.

Jared tilted his head and stared at her in bewilderment, half expecting her to rip off her bra and twirl it around overhead. "Is this supposed to be fun or something?" he asked as they walked up to the porch.

"Of course it is," Deborah said. "It's a party. There's going to be presents and games and—"

"Are we going to play pin the dead fetus in the womb?" Jared asked.

Deborah punched him on the shoulder, the pile of presents slipping out of her hands and spilling onto the sidewalk.

"Look what you did," Jared said before Deborah could blame him. "The wrapping paper is wrinkled now. And look at that bow in disarray. We can't present these presents."

Jared laughed especially hard at his last line.

Deborah punched him again and told him to pick them up. "You better not embarrass me," she said, accompanying her words with her best death stare.

Jared didn't die. "Too late," he said, pointing to the front door where Sherry and her husband were standing, ready to open the door and invite their guests inside. Or ready to collect their loot, Jared thought as he bent down to pick up the gifts and help his wife save face.

"Congratulations!" Jared shouted with his arms full of the gifts. "I couldn't be happier for you!"

Deborah shot him a look. He apparently was over the top.

"Yes," Deborah said. "We are indeed happy for you."

Jared handed the happy un-expectant couple the gifts and waited for their "thank yous" to be delivered. They took the gifts like piranhas with greedy hands but said nothing.

With mangled gifts in hand, Sherry and her husband welcomed the couple inside.

"You're the first ones here," Sherry declared in an honorific tone. "You can have a seat in the hearth room until everyone else arrives. There's drinks waiting for you. Please use a coaster."

Deborah smiled and led her husband into the hearth room.

"What the hell's a hearth room?" Jared asked when they sat down, looking around to see why it was so special. He didn't have a hearth room in his house, and he wondered why his room wasn't good enough for such a title.

"It's a room with a nice fireplace. Look how beautiful their fireplace is." She walked over to the fireplace and rubbed her hand along the bricks. Jared knew she didn't know what she was talking about, but he didn't bother to tell her what he knew.

"Oh, and don't be a jerk," she added after her inspection of the bricks seemed complete and satisfactory.

"What are you talking about?"

"Your tone out there was obnoxious. You don't have to mock them."

"I wasn't mocking anyone. I was just treating them like I would anyone else celebrating a momentous occasion." He looked around again. "Where the hell are those drinks they were talking about?"

"Over there," Deborah said, pointing to a big cooler.

Jared rose from the couch and glanced in the cooler. Nothing but light beer. "I'd rather drink piss," he muttered and flopped back on the couch.

"No one's stopping you," she responded.

"You'd probably say I was embarrassing you."

"It would be embarrassing if my husband starting drinking piss in front of everyone at a party," she said, staring at the doorway.

"Well, this is one hell of a party. I wouldn't want to embarrass you at such a fine event."

Before she could respond, Tony and Drake walked in giggling with their hands clasped tightly. They both wore plaid shirts and tight colored pants. Jared cringed at their flamboyance. He didn't care that they were gay, but they could at least wear normal pants.

"Deborah, Jared, wonderful to see you!" Drake shouted as he released Tony's hand and scuttled over to Deborah. He planted a kiss on each cheek and then turned and pretended to do the same to Jared.

"It's wonderful to see you too," Deborah said. Jared rolled his eyes at her false enthusiasm. He knew she didn't think much of them. He was convinced she actually hated gay people. She at least was against gay marriage, a topic that didn't bother Jared. As long as it didn't affect his ability to do anything, it didn't matter to him.

"So, aren't you just so happy for Sherry?" Tony said to Jared, plopping down on the couch a little too close for Jared's comfort.

Although Jared didn't want to, he made small talk with Tony for a few minutes while the other guests filed into the room, carrying various gift bags and bottles of liquor. The room buzzed with happiness as everyone gushed over how great Sherry looked.

"Yeah, she looks great," Jared said, even though he didn't think she looked any better now than she ever had. He didn't know how far along she'd made it into the pregnancy, but surely not enough to gain any weight. Hell, he knew of women who *lost* weight during the first trimester. If anything, Sherry should look better now than she ever had before.

Just when Jared didn't think he could take all the nonsense anymore, someone announced it was time for the gifts. Apparently they were on a tight schedule. They had to make sure the gifts were all opened and the cake and alcohol was all consumed before some big finale.

"What's this finale?" Jared whispered to his wife, but she turned away from him with a terse "Shhh." Jared figured she was still mad about the supposed scene he'd caused upon entry. He was sure he'd hear nothing but nagging about that for the next month.

As much as Jared didn't want to be there, he was curious about what kind of gifts everyone had brought. And of course he wanted to know what the hell the big finale was all about.

The first few gifts were pretty boring. A gift card for a massage. A pair of comfy slippers. A gym membership. Jared had no idea what to expect at such event, but he figured the gifts would at least be fun. Soon enough, they were.

Everyone watched in suspense as Sherry opened a long box and pulled out a silver studded dildo. Jared's eyes popped at the sight of the massive phallus. It must've been over a foot long with the girth of a beer can.

"What the hell's she supposed to do with that?" Jared whispered to some woman's husband sitting next to him on the couch. The husband shrugged and glanced at his wife. She shook her head and the man said nothing in response to Jared. The man didn't even look at him again.

For the next dozen or so gifts, the crowd really went wild, laughing and applauding the great gifts poured upon the happy couple. Most of the gifts seemed specifically for Sherry, although there was a mega box of condoms that was arguably just as much for the husband. "Maybe we wouldn't all be here if they'd just thought to wear condoms before," Jared muttered to no one in particular. No one bothered to pay attention, if they heard him at all.

When all the gifts were finally opened, the cake was distributed and the liquor was poured. Everyone ate and drank in a hurry, and a sense of unease began to sweep through the room. Jared figured it was just the result of calorie counting and indigestion.

Before the last bottle could be emptied, the doorbell rang.

"He's here," someone said, followed by a few nervous oooohs.

One of the women rushed to the door while everyone else chugged the last of their drinks. When the woman returned a few moments later, a man wearing a white coat and carrying a black briefcase followed her. The guy almost looked like a doctor, but he looked more like a medical school dropout than an accomplished doctor.

"What's the doctor doing here?" Jared asked his wife, forming his fingers into air quotes on the word "doctor."

"What do you mean?" she asked.

"Why is there a doctor here?"

"Are you being serious?"

"Yes. What the hell is going on? Is he going to examine her?"

She stared at him, and he felt dumb for some reason unknown to him, which made him feel even dumber.

"Well, what's the deal?" he asked when she didn't bother answering.

"He's here to do the operation," she hissed. "Now stop embarrassing me. Just shut up and watch."

"Wait a minute. You said they didn't do it here."

"Well, I lied. I knew you would object to the whole thing if I told you."

"You're damn right I would've objected. You mean he's going to do the abortion right here in front of all of us?" Jared squealed. Whereas his previous remarks were wholly ignored by the crowd, everyone stared at him now, many with glares of disgust.

Deborah slapped Jared on the shoulder. "What's the matter with you?" she yelled at him.

Jared stood up. "What's the matter with *me*? *I'm* not the one celebrating a live abortion. How can you people intend to watch this?"

The guests chattered their support for Sherry and their hatred for Jared. There were so many flapping voices that Jared couldn't really decipher a word.

Amidst the drama, the doctor popped open his briefcase and took out some menacing tools. "I think this would be better without him here," the doctor said while pointing a long sharp instrument at Jared.

"I don't plan to stay," Jared said as he began heading for the door.

As he walked out, he could hear Deborah's apologies. "I'm so sorry. He's just backwards. He doesn't understand the way the world is today. And he's had a lot of stress at work. He doesn't mean it. He—"

Jared decided he couldn't listen to her rambling justifications any longer. He stopped and began shouting without turning around. "There's nothing wrong with my view of the world. You're the ones in the wrong." He swung around, an outstretched finger condemning all of the guests in a sweeping gesture. "I don't care what you do in the privacy of the doctor's office, but to invite people to this is barbaric. It's like you're turning this into a human sacrifice."

"I'm not sacrificing anything," Sherry said. "I'm actually liberating myself. I'm doing the opposite of sacrificing."

"Go ahead and think that if you want," Jared said.

"I have the right to think whatever I want. And I have the right to do whatever I want in my own home," Sherry said.

"Somebody get this asshole out of here," the doctor said while observing his collection of tools once more.

"No one needs to force me out. I'm out on my own." He looked at Deborah before he left. She was obviously mortified. "Don't expect to find me at home tonight," he said to her. "I can't be with anyone who involves herself in such a ridiculous event."

Deborah began sobbing in her hands and a group of women comforted her.

"We really must do this," the doctor said. "I have several other parties to get to this afternoon."

Jared spit on the floor and left. He cursed everyone all the way to the car, and continued to let out his hateful strings of profanity on the drive home to pack his things.

Back home, Jared rushed through the house with a suitcase. As he gathered the few possessions he felt were worth keeping, he spotted a used pregnancy test in the trashcan. Pulling it out with shaking hands, he did his best to decipher the markings on the stick. It was negative. He sighed and slid to the floor. He wasn't sure what the hell he'd do if his wife was actually having a baby. Once he was able to stand, he said a little prayer of thanks that there was no baby on the way. He didn't want to have to deal with such an inconvenience, especially not at a time like this.

A Blade of Love

Allan Thermoose's wife is in love with a blade of grass. It's the 375th blade directly even with the crack in the third slab of sidewalk east of the mailbox. The blade gets full sun all day, and Allan, a stickler for lawn maintenance, is careful to water it, along with all the others, for approximately thirty minutes per day, moving the sprinkler three times to ensure even water distribution. He occasionally counts the residual droplets left on the tufts of grass fifteen minutes after he shuts off the water. If he's not happy with the results, he repeats the process until he's positive his lawn has had enough to drink. None of this is done for his wife.

Allan knows he shouldn't be worried about his wife's newfound love. It can't last, he tells himself. It's just a blade of grass. It will probably die in the winter (although he hopes it comes back in the spring). Besides, it's not like she can get married to it, and the blade certainly can't provide for her. Every once in a while Allan considers doing something extra nice for his wife to compete with the piece of lawn, but he shouldn't need to compete for his own wife's love. Besides, the way he cares for the lawn should be enough.

The blade of grass is in the center of the lawn. It first caught Mrs. Thermoose's eye on a Tuesday when she was out getting the mail. There was an electric bill, two catalogs, and one of those things asking for money for kids with cleft lips. Although the pictures of those kids frightened her, she always sent a check to them anyway. Maybe that's why she sent the check. She was positive that the grass winked at her. She wasn't sure on the way out, but as she walked back, mail in hand, sundress lightly dangling off her soft frame, she was almost sure of it. Whether it was a wink or not, the look it gave her made her feel something that Allan hadn't made her feel in quite some time. Allan wouldn't have even noticed the type of dress she wore. The grass did.

She waited three weeks before telling Allan about her feelings. She did it right when he walked in the door from work, before he had the chance to put out the sprinklers for the day. Allan hadn't even set down his briefcase yet. "Sit down," she had told him.

"I sit all day. Besides, it's time to water the grass," he responded.

"I'm in love with someone else," she said.

"Who?" he asked while trying to decide if he should keep holding the briefcase. He did.

"You'll laugh," she told him, "but it's serious. We're in love."

"I won't laugh. Tell me who it is." Allan set down the briefcase and thought about whether or not he should go to his wife. He didn't.

She told him.

His initial reaction was to laugh, but something about the way she spoke told him she was either serious or crazy. He had wondered why she was spending so much time outside. She used to hate the outdoors but now it seemed like all she did was stand in the center of the lawn staring at the ground. Allan never even thought to ask her what she was doing. It all made sense once she told him, at least to some extent. He wondered if he was to blame. Certainly it was his fault that the blade was so enticing, although he wasn't even sure at that point which blade it was. He couldn't think of anything he'd done to push her into such lunacy.

"Aren't you going to say anything?" she asked after a while.

"I need to go mow the lawn," he said.

"No you don't. It's Wednesday. You don't mow on Wednesday." She looked frightened at the thought of the lawn being mowed.

"Then I need to water it," he told her.

She watched from the window when he went out to water the grass. He eyed her occasionally as he walked around the lawn and deposited the sprinkler in all the usual places. He wondered if she was watching him or staring at her grass. While he was out there he thought he saw a blade wink at him, but then he felt the breeze that must've caused it. "Why would any of the grass love *her* anyway?" he asked out loud as he tried to figure out which one was the culprit.

It took quite a bit of time to figure out which one she loved. They all looked the same to him, but that might be because he spends so much time making sure that each blade of grass is perfect. The only ones he ever notices are the inferior ones, which he pulls out almost immediately if they are standing alone. If they're grouped, he has a different approach that takes a great deal more time. There are no inferior ones around hers. Just a perfect plot of grass. He had to count out the blades at least a dozen times before he pinpointed her exact love. For some reason she was reluctant at first to point it out to him. "You'll know it when you see it," she always told him.

Allan stares at the lawn in a different way now. He used to admire it. Now he is trying to figure it out. Of course he still cares for it just as well. It gets as much water as it did before, and he cuts it on the same schedule. The only difference is how much he looks at it. Often when he is outside a neighbor will stroll by and compliment him on such fine lawn care. They are always in awe that he doesn't pay anyone to treat it. Why would he pay when he can do it himself? Allan nods a thank you and goes back to looking at the grass. The neighbors think he is searching for imperfections and tell him to relax. He doesn't tell them why he can't, so he chuckles an awkward chuckle and continues to study it. No matter how much he stares though he just can't figure out what she sees in that particular blade. After giving it a few dozen looks, he can't help but think it looks a little dull compared to some of its neighbors. He wonders why it isn't the 223rd blade just east of the center of the elm's trunk. Now *that* is a beautiful piece of grass.

Allan is under strict instruction not to cut his wife's blade of grass anymore. If he trims it even a centimeter, she's asking for a divorce—and she may even call the cops. He tells her he isn't going to mow that patch of grass, but this is not acceptable. Her blade must stand out above all others, so he has to trim all the grass around it by hand, making sure not to harm hers in any way. He asks if he can mark it somehow to be sure he doesn't accidentally cut it, possibly with a little paint, but she says no, the blade won't like that very much at all. "Can I at least put a toothpick in the ground next to it?" he asks her. Even that is too much. She thinks it will hurt the roots. Allan understands her point and wishes he hadn't suggested such a thing in the first place.

She's taken to sleeping outside three days a week to be closer to her love. She snuggles with it and gives it kisses in the morning. She pretends the drops of dew are the blade kissing her back. Allan begs her to wait until after sundown to lie with the grass and to come back in before the sun comes up. She obeys his first request but not his second. Each of those mornings she comes in with damp garments and a bare shoulder. He's thinking of installing an automated sprinkler system that will douse her at four in the morning, but he wonders if maybe she wouldn't enjoy this a little too much.

It's late spring and Allan wants to fertilize, but his wife says her blade doesn't want that. He insists it will help the grass grow to its fullest potential, but she, knowing nothing about lawn care, thinks applying any foreign substances will make it lose its sparkle. She's been keeping her makeup on at night and wearing lacey nightgowns to give a little extra sparkle to herself. She only does this on the nights she spends outside of course. When she stays inside with Allan she dons a baggy nightshirt and a bare face. Allan shrugs at bedtime each night and wonders why she ever bothers to stay in.

Her blade is now seven inches tall. City code requires lawns to be no longer than six inches, but the city isn't going to get involved over a single piece of too-long grass. Allan almost calls the city himself to report it but he doesn't want to pay the fine or waste the tax dollars on the investigation. The grass all around is only three inches. She is now insisting that the rest of the grass needs to be cut down to two inches. He thinks the single tall blade is unsightly and wishes his wife would forget about this crush. Two inch grass is ugly anyway. Allan never did enjoy walking past those buzzed lawns.

His neighbors ask about the abnormally long bit of grass. He tells them he missed a spot. They ask if he's okay. He's never missed a spot before and now he seems to miss the same spot every week. Allan can't tell them about his wife's feelings. They'll think she's insane which means he's insane. Truth is he's embarrassed about the whole thing. He'd rather his wife be in love with another man.

On Sunday, as usual, Allan mows the lawn. He likes to do the crisscross pattern, except around the trees where he cuts a three-tiered circle. Of course he leaves the small patch in the middle with that one extra-long blade. When he is finished mowing he walks to the center of the yard with a small pair of scissors and trims each strand with barber-like precision to match the rest of the lawn. He contemplates cutting his wife's blade. He opens the scissors and slides them next to the single tall piece of grass. The scissors hover there waiting to close on the blade that towers over everything else. No one is around. He starts to push the metal blades together. They are a mere centimeters away from each other when he hears the grass whisper, "I love her." He removes the scissors and tells it to treat her well. Then he goes and cleans the gutters. From the roof he watches his wife go outside and sit with the grass. She looks happy and he smiles as he removes a clump of leaves and tosses it to the ground below. He looks at the leaves longingly and wonders if any of them could fall in love with him. They just stare back all crumply and dead.

Dead Man Sleeping

Joyce Addleberg hated sleeping alone, so when her husband died in his sleep one night, it was only natural that she kept him around.

At first, even though he was cold and stiff, he provided her with the warmth and companionship she needed.

But soon, and it settled in slowly, his body began to emit a rather unpleasant smell. It was a mere distraction at first, but she soon found sleeping next to him almost impossible. She began going to bed with a doctor's mask covering her nose and mouth, but the putrid smell quickly found a way to penetrate the thin fabric.

She started to think that preservation was in order, to at least make the man tolerable again. She thought of formaldehyde, but her knowledge in the usage of such substances was limited, so she decided to seek the assistance of a professional. She called a local taxidermy.

"Hello, Frank's Taxidermy, covering all your needs for the last thirty years," a man she assumed to be Frank answered.

"Yes, how much to stuff my husband?" she asked.

"Excuse me?" Frank seemed genuinely surprised.

"I would like to stuff my husband. He's about 5'10" and 170 pounds, if that helps."

"Lady, I hope you're joking," Frank said before hanging up.

"Well, he certainly didn't cover my needs," she said before scanning the phonebook for a more reputable-sounding business. Surely someone could meet her needs, even if Frank couldn't.

But no one could, so she simply masked the odor with an assortment of plug-in air fresheners and sprays.

She continued to sleep next to her rotting husband, but their relationship quickly changed. She no longer offered him a kiss before bed, and she didn't tuck his decaying arm around her fragile skin. After a while, she didn't even sleep under the covers with him, keeping as much distance as she could.

Soon, she met someone else to take to bed, a man with a similar build to her dead husband's, a man she met at the grocery store while loading up on ice cream and air fresheners. Of course, when he came home with her, she hid her husband underneath the bed, fully aware that this new suitor would probably not become a permanent replacement.

"What is that awful smell?" he asked the first time they made love.

"It's my past," she told him.

"Well, perhaps we best do this at my place from now on."

Joyce nodded her head in agreement as they prepared to make love again.

When the suitor left in the morning, Joyce apologized to her husband's body as she pulled it out from underneath the bed. She felt terrible as she looked upon the rotting corpse, now covered in cobwebs and dust bunnies. She vowed to him that she would vacuum under the bed before placing him there again. To make it up to him, she allowed him to spoon her that night. The curious smile on his sunken face in the morning told her that he had forgiven her, and he didn't even complain when she resorted back to treating him like a leper the next night.

Three nights later, Joyce's new suitor, Bradley Hemperden, requested dinner and a movie at his place, and suggested she bring something comfortable for sleeping. She gladly acquiesced to his requests. However, Joyce did little sleeping that night at Bradley's place. A terrible fear arose in her that her husband might not only be hurt by her sleeping with another man, but he might also be very lonely. She tossed and turned almost the entire night, wishing that she could exchange the warmth of this man for the cold grasp of her husband's festering arm.

In the morning, Joyce said to Bradley, "I'm sorry, but I can't do this anymore."

Bradley stared, his mouth agape, as if wondering how any woman whose home smelled so foul could possibly reject an opportunity to sleep with him at his chic loft.

"Say something," she said after the silent staring grew uncomfortable.

"Okay, then we can go back to your place, I suppose," Bradley told her with an eagerness that suggested she satisfied his sexual needs quite satisfactorily.

"No, no, I mean, I can't do this with you anymore. The sleeping together thing. It's just not right."

"I'm confused," Bradley stated. "You were so eager to jump into bed together the other night, and you came running as soon as I beckoned *last* night. What's the problem?"

"I'm married," she said with a blush of shame.

"Where was your husband the other night?"

"Under the bed."

Again, Bradley gave her that open mouth stare.

"Say something."

This time, Bradley had nothing to say.

"Relax," she said. "He's not alive anymore."

"Oh," he responded, sounding rather relieved. "So you keep his ashes under your bed?"

"His ashes? Heavens, no. Frederick would never go for cremation."

"Then what precisely is under your bed?" He sounded nervous but looked surprisingly calm.

"Well..." she began.

"You mean..." His face began to turn green.

"I'm afraid so. Obviously, you understand that I must end this, for Frederick's sake."

"You know what you are doing is illegal, right?"

"Goodness, why would it be illegal? He's my husband. I'm rather sure he's quite happy where he is."

"But how do you deal with the smell?"

Looking at Bradley, Joyce wondered why the man would even converse with her, but it occurred to her that this couldn't really be any worse than any of his previous lovers' flaws. Deep down, in fact, he must deem her behavior commendable. After all, one had to admire such lasting fidelity, and that's all Joyce really was — a good and faithful woman.

"Oh, you get used to it, I suppose. It was rather difficult sleeping next to him at first, but I've grown accustomed to it. On the bright side, he doesn't disturb me in the middle of the night like he used to, and he never tries to get frisky with me when I'm not in the mood." She beamed with pride at the thought of her lovely husband.

"But don't you miss those things? They always say that it's the little things about someone that really get you. What does he really have going for him now?"

Joyce thought about it for a while before settling on, "He's my husband. He's the only one I've ever had. He's the only one I ever want." Tears swelled in her eyes. She hadn't cried since he died, and she felt embarrassed now for doing it in front of this man.

"It's okay, Joyce, I'm here for you now. And I always will be, if you'll let me," he told her as he held her hand and wiped a tear from her cheek.

Joyce stared at Bradley, trying to evaluate what exactly he wanted. He was certainly a strikingly handsome man, and he seemed rather sincere in his intentions. He must obviously care for her since he didn't run screaming when she told him that she slept with her dead husband. Although she found it comforting, it was rather odd. In fact, it was downright disturbing that this man, whom she had only known for a few days, was so desperate that he wanted to share her bed with a dead man. And then her thoughts drifted back to that lonely bed back home.

"I'm sorry, Bradley," she said. "I must go home to my Frederick. He's so lonely and he's been so good to me. I've been a terrible wife the last few days."

Joyce could tell by the look in his eyes that he understood her feelings, but was hurt that she preferred a rotting corpse over him. He planted a gentle kiss on her cheek and let her go.

When Joyce returned home, she breathed in deeply, but her husband's distinct smell had virtually vanished. In a panic she rushed to the bedroom to make sure he was still there. There he was indeed, in the precise spot she had left him, but somehow he didn't look as rotten. In fact, he looked almost as good as he had before he died. With a warm smile, she planted a kiss on his lips and curled up next to him for the rest of the day, promising him that she would never sleep with another man as long as she lived. She had everything she needed in a husband right at her side, and for that, she was eternally grateful.

The Arrival

Everybody knew it would happen. It didn't happen exactly when or how they thought it would, but nonetheless it happened.

"I told you it would happen," a bearded man told his wife.

"Of course you did. Everyone knew it would happen," the wife responded while thinking he could use a nice shave. He would be a lot more handsome with a shave.

"Well, I knew how it would happen, too," he said through the massive piles of wiry brown hair that surrounded his mouth.

"No you didn't. No one did. If someone had, then it could have been delayed," she said, trying to picture his face hairless.

"Well, at least I knew when it would happen," the beard said.

"No you didn't. No one did. If someone had, then we would have been prepared." All she could see now was a giant mound of hair talking to her.

On a certain level, everyone was relieved when it finally did happen. They had been waiting a long time for it. Finally, they could relax. There was no reason for anxiety anymore.

Some had doubted at first, but the source of their doubt was likely rooted in denial. Everyone came around eventually. Luckily, by the time it did happen, no one seemed to doubt it anymore.

"What should we wear?" the wife asked the beard.

"It doesn't matter," the beard responded.

"But it might be the last thing we get to wear." She was genuinely concerned, both about her outfit and her husband's raggedy appearance.

"Then wear something you like," spewed out the parted patches of brown hair.

There was a lot of variety in dress that day. Some chose to look their finest. Others sought clothing that they found comfortable. Still others tried to make one final fashion statement that set themselves apart. Regardless, everyone changed clothes when they found out it had happened. The bearded man had been right though. It didn't really matter as long as you didn't show up naked.

"Should we eat before we go?" the worried wife wondered.

"The impression I get is that the food shall be plentiful. We shan't ever hunger again," the beard spoke as the stomach below rumbled.

"Should we have a snack just in case?"

"Perhaps we had better."

She hoped that no crumbs would stick in the mess of mouth hair.

Most people ate a snack before they left. It happened halfway between lunch and dinner, and people were starting to get a little hungry. The snack would tide them over until dinner. Most assumed dinner would be served a little late. With all those people, it would be difficult to serve everyone efficiently. No one considered that dinner might not be served. Everyone just expected it. Just the event itself, they weren't sure when or how, but they knew it would happen.

"Should we bring anything with us?" the beard parted to ask.

"I'm not sure. I don't think we need anything, but perhaps we should bring a few essentials just in case," the wife said, adding *Perhaps you should bring a razor* to herself.

"What are the essentials?" the beard wondered, hoping a razor wasn't among them.

"Well, we need toothpaste, deodorant, soap, clean underwear, makeup, and..." she paused. "Maybe a razor and some toilet paper. You know, the things we can't live without."

"Can we really bring all that?" he wondered.

The wife didn't respond. She was too busy putting all the essentials in a bag.

No one was really sure whether or not they should bring something. It seemed likely they should. They would likely never return to their homes. Some people brought practical things. Some brought sentimental things. Some, those who were very confident about their fate, brought nothing but themselves.

"What time should we arrive?" the woman asked frantically as she ran around the house filling the bag.

"I think we should try to arrive early," the beard flapped.

"When should we leave?" The bag was overflowing.

"Probably now," he said before she had had time to pack the razor.

Everyone arrived early. None of them knew what exactly to expect other than huge crowds and hopefully eternal happiness. They stood in throngs, barely room between each other to distinguish where one life form ended and a new one began. They talked among themselves, but the conversations were mostly meaningless and found themselves lost in other conversations.

They waited for a long time before the man they could hear but not see spoke to them. "All who are presentable but not magnificent, hungry but not empty, prepared but not equipped, early but not premature may enter."

The crowd looked amongst itself, each member wondering if he or she met these requirements. No one spoke with their mouths, instead just offering each other puzzled looks. The silence of death hung over the crowd.

They were still looking at each other two hours later when the gates closed.

Living with a Giant Squid

My daughter told me there was a giant squid under her bed. She told me this many times. I always assumed she was just telling me this because we went to Sea World and saw a giant squid and she thought it was scary, so she imagined there was one in her room to get some extra attention. She said it so many times my wife begged me to go up and check even though the very notion of a giant squid fitting under her bed was completely and utterly ridiculous.

"Your bed is so small," I told her. "How could something so big live there?"

"It rolls itself into a little ball," she said with such certainty I thought maybe it had just snuck into our belongings and made its way home with us.

I still refused to check, mainly out of principle. "There's nothing to worry about. Besides, the giant squid would need water to live."

Which of course made her panic because now there was a dying giant squid under her bed.

When she was at school the next day, I left work early to go home and peek under the bed. There it was, all balled up, a giant squid. But it didn't look like it was dying.

"It's okay little fella," I said to it, but it wouldn't come out of its ball. It actually seemed to tighten itself. "Fine, suit yourself," I told it and went off to take a shower.

A few minutes later a tentacle crept into the shower and took the bar of soap right as I was reaching for it.

I asked for the soap back and maybe for a little privacy if it didn't mind. I didn't expect the squid to respond, but he did.

"I'd like some more water and maybe a few hundred minnows a day," he told me. I couldn't see his face, but it sounded like he wasn't really asking.

"I can't give you those things," I stammered even though deep down I couldn't believe the squid was the one talking to me. "Just give me the soap please."

"I'm afraid I can't do that until you've met my demands," it responded. Its voice was much higher than I expected from a giant underwater creature.

"That's fine. We've got plenty more soap," I told him as I pulled the curtain open and reached for the cabinet. Before I could even grab the handle the squid opened the cabinet and took all the soap. Then he swiped a few more tentacles out and took my towel, my razor, my shampoo, and a few other items. I never realized how many tentacles a squid had, and I certainly wasn't able to count them in that moment, but there sure were a lot of them. I also knew I didn't want to get out of the shower without washing up first, so I told the squid I'd give everything he wanted if he just gave me the soap.

"I'm not sure I trust you," he told me.

"You have my word," I said and offered him a hand to shake. Somehow I knew he could see me even if I couldn't see his face. He wrapped a long thin tentacle around my hand and shook it quickly. I expected the shake to be slimier. I'd touched used car salesmen with more slime.

He returned a sliver of soap and told me he had an eye on me even though I couldn't see it. I imagined him squinting his eyes and pointing at me.

I hurried and washed my body, always looking back expecting the squid to reach a tentacle around me and suffocate me before hopping into the shower and living happily ever after, but he really did leave me alone just as I had originally asked. The squid had better manners than I had anticipated. I wondered if it was a common trait of squids.

After I finished with the shower I toweled off and went to the store to pick up a few things. I asked the squid if he wanted to come along but he told me he was afraid of cars.

It took quite some time to amass a big enough collection of water and minnows to satisfy the squid. I had to visit six pet shops before I had what could even pass for a hundred of the little fish.

The squid seemed quite pleased with my purchases. I was worried he would count the minnows and tell me there weren't a hundred, but he just accepted them, gobbling up half of them with one swallow.

"Those aren't half bad," he told me, but I could tell he thought they were more than half bad. I left him alone in his new pool filled with water under the bed. I had to raise my daughter's bed a little to fit the thing under there, but I figured she wouldn't really noticed.

When she returned home from school, the scream alerted me to the fact that she didn't like the little change I had made to her room. The squid screamed right back, his louder and higher than hers.

"What's the matter?" I asked in a panic after I sprinted up the stairs to their room.

"She screamed at me," the squid said. I don't think my daughter heard him.

"See. There's a squid under my bed," my daughter said with a firm point. "And now he has a little pool. He's going to pull me in there and drown me while I sleep."

"Squidsy will do no such thing," I instantly replied. The squid gave me an odd look, and I knew I should have consulted him before bestowing a moniker upon him.

"The name is Charles," the squid said with a disgusted look. "Squidsy? Seriously? That's the best you could do."

"You *named* him?" my daughter said in an appalled voice.

"Yes, but apparently the name I gave him isn't good enough."

"It is a pretty dumb name," Charles said. My daughter gave no sign she agreed.

"Can't you get rid of it, Daddy?" she pleaded.

"Sorry, sweetie. You're just going to have to share your room now. I think you and Charles will get along pretty well," I insisted. She turned up her nose and stormed out of the room.

"Women," I said to Charles, but Charles either didn't acknowledge my comment or didn't understand. I guess he didn't have much experience with the ladies in his underwater days.

Within a few seconds my wife marched into the room with my daughter in tow.

"Our daughter is not sharing a room with that thing," she said from the doorway, my daughter clinging to her legs.

"Well, we can't really give him his own room," I shot back. "We don't have the space for that."

"Then we'll just have to get rid of it," my wife ordered.

"We can't just throw him out on the street. Who would take care of him? You don't do that kind of thing to a member of the family." I wasn't sure why I had become so attached to Charles. Maybe I just didn't like being bossed around. Regardless of the reason, I wasn't going to give him up.

"Then you can share the basement with it," she said with her coldest death stare. I glanced back at Charles and saw him curled up into the tightest ball imaginable. The water in his pool looked like it was about to freeze under the wrathful gaze of my wife. I shivered at the thought of Charles suffering in that icy water.

"We will not go to the basement," I roared at her. "Charles will stay right here, and I will sleep in my bed. If you don't like it, you can go to the basement."

Charles uncurled himself and placed a thankful tentacle on my shoulder. I patted it and shot him a quick smile. I couldn't quite tell, but I was pretty sure he reciprocated.

My wife huffed in frustration and pulled my daughter away, pulling the door shut behind her and leaving me alone with Charles.

"Like I said before, women," I said with a roll of your eyes.

Charles stroked my shoulder for a moment and then brought up a handful of tentacles to work the knots out of my back.

"Not all women are bad," Charles said while working his magic.

"Name one that's not."

"I'm not."

I laughed. "You're not a woman."

"Of course I am."

"But your name is Charles," I squeaked.

"Yeah, so."

"And you're so big."

"Actually, females are bigger than males in my species. We typically have stronger names because of that." Charles continued to dig her tentacles into the loosening muscles of my back.

"Is that a fact?" I asked in a state of perfect peace I hadn't felt in years.

"Do you have any reason not to trust me?" she asked. It didn't take more than a few seconds of thinking to realize I had none.

Charles and I slept in my daughter's room that night. Eliza never came in, not even to get any of her stuff. I slept there the next night as well. My wife and daughter avoided me at all costs during those two days, so I decided it was time for Charles and me to get our own place.

"Charles and I are getting our own place," I told my wife when I happened upon her while I was packing my clothes in our former bedroom.

"That's stupid," she said. "I can't believe you are choosing a squid over your family."

"Charles gets me. She knows what I want. We've got a little place in the city lined up."

"You're moving to the city with a giant squid?" she said.

"Yeah. You got a problem with that." I wanted to throw my arms out to challenge her, but I knew it wouldn't be much of a challenge.

"Good luck," she said before storming out. I could tell she was just jealous.

The first week went okay, with Charles giving me massages every night and I giving her baths. On the eighth day I started to realize that we never really talked about anything.

"So how many tentacles do you have anyway?" I asked her.

"How should I know? Squids can't count."

"Why are they called *ten*tacles if you have more than ten?"

"I don't think that *ten* is a prefix there."

"Why did you decide to leave the ocean?"

"To get away from annoyances," she said with a sharp look. I stopped asking questions then and there. I wondered if this was all a big mistake. Perhaps humans and squids weren't meant to share a life together.

"I'll take you back to the ocean if you want," I told her.

"Nope. I'm good here." Then she curled up into a little ball and stayed there for the next three days. During those three days she didn't eat or say a thing, and although the quiet was nice, it really made me focus on how much she stunk. Giving her all those baths must've warded off the awful decaying ocean scent, but unbathed, she was just unbearable.

Finally, on the fourth day when she rolled out of the ball and glanced at me, I told her that it was over and that I was going home.

"That's nice," she said.

"What will you do?"

"Stay here."

"How will you pay for it?"

"Squids don't need money," she said confidently. "I'll manage," she added when she noticed my worried look.

When I returned home that very night, my wife and daughter gave me the cold shoulder at first, but after a few hours they just couldn't hold back their curiosity.

"So what's it like living with a giant squid?" they asked.

"Let's just say I have no desire to go to the ocean anytime soon," I told them. We all shared a hearty chuckle even though I didn't think there was anything funny about what we said. I washed out Eliza's room and had some decent sex with my wife that night.

The next day I drove to the city apartment and tried to check in on Charles, but she didn't answer when I knocked. I came back the next three days, but she never answered. On the fourth day, the landlord asked me what I was doing and demanded I stay off his property unless I could honor the lease. I gave him the year's worth of rent right then and there and told him to take good care of Charles. He told me I was crazy but gladly took my money.

A month later I saw what looked like a giant squid wearing a trench coat enter a pet store. I would've followed her, but I was running late for a date with my wife. We were going to a seafood restaurant with the best calamari in town. We had wanted to go there for quite a long time.

Quitting is Easy

I took up smoking just to show the world how easy it was to quit. It's been five months now, and my wife is wondering why I haven't yet.

"It takes time baby. I have to develop the addiction first," I tell her.

"Please stop," she begs me. "It's so gross I don't even want to kiss you anymore."

I can verify this statement. I'm not sure when the last time we shared a good passionate kiss, the kind where we slap our tongues around the other's mouth.

"Look, I'll quit soon. I just need to make sure that I'm addicted. Otherwise it's too easy to quit and I won't have proven my point."

"And exactly who are you proving this point to again?" she asks with a roll of her beautiful green eyes. It looks like sea foam bouncing around on flawless shores. For a moment I think about quitting just so I can kiss her, but my willpower is too strong. I can't give into temptation.

"Honey, this is our ticket to millions," I plead with her as I reach for the carton of cigarettes on top of the fridge.

"And how is that exactly?"

I have to pause here. I don't always think through exactly where I am headed with something, but I'm always convinced that I'll get to where I want to go. Nothing comes to me, and I don't want to seem like I'm racking my brain too much, so I just go with my gut.

"Don't worry about it. You'll see it when it happens. I can't give away all my secrets." I am tempted to go on a little longer, but any more than that and she will know for sure I'm stalling.

"You're stalling," she says.

I light my cigarette and take a deep drag.

"Hey, I told you not to do that in the house. Get the hell out of here with that. Do you want the walls and furniture to turn yellow?" She waves her arms frantically in the air as if to ward off some evil.

"Relax, I'll put it out." I put it out just to show her how easy it's going to be for me to quit. My hand almost immediately begins to shake.

"I want you to stop by the end of the week. Stop or I'm leaving you." The sea foam is gone from her eyes. They're acidic now.

"Hey, look how easy it was for me to put that out." I put my shaking hand behind my back. "Look, I think the addiction has just about fully kicked in." I wrap my arms around her to show what a great husband I am. "I've never been addicted to anything after just one time."

Oops. She immediately pulls out of my grip and shoots me a death stare. I can feel her eyes burn though me. The look is almost as bad as the need for a cigarette. I know what she wants me to say, but saying it now will only make her appear to be happy. It's one of her many tricks. She makes me say something because she's angry, then she pretends to be happy, but I can sense that she is even more upset because she thinks I only said it because she wanted me to say it, which is apparently worse than not saying it at all.

"I'm going shopping," she says to interrupt my thoughts. I don't bother to tell her what she wants to hear. I'm just thankful that she's getting out of the house. My veins feel like they'll collapse if I don't get some nicotine in my system right away.

"Alrighty, babe. Need me to do anything while you're gone?"

"Yeah. Just one thing. Don't smoke."

"Fine. I won't smoke. I'll just throw everything I've started away."

"Good. Throw that damn carton away while you're at it." She turns on her heel and marches for the front door without bothering to tell me where she's going or when she'll return. I know I'm supposed to ask, but I know she won't tell me when I do. Either way she'll be mad, so I might as well just save face. I don't want to look weak in front of the cigarettes.

I hear the door slam and my shaking hand immediately reaches for the carton. I have to be honest here. The cigarettes took their full affect about two months ago. It's been like a disease ever since. If Amy knew how many cartons I was plowing through then she would at least take away my credit cards and kick me in the balls. Amy would never divorce me, for any reason. Her parents divorced when she was a teenager, and she despises divorce more than anything, even more than smoking. Still, I'm not going to tempt her too much, so I grab a pack out of the carton and head for the backyard. She'll know I was smoking, but at least if I do it back here then she'll pretend she doesn't know.

She won't even act pissy or give the impression that she thinks I'm hiding something. As long as it doesn't seem to affect her, she really doesn't mind.

I light the cigarette before I even get outside. I wait until the door is halfway closed before I take my first puff. It's an instant feeling of relief. I may have become addicted to sex a lot quicker, but the rush of smoke into my lungs and veins defeats any orgasm I've ever had. I always used to wonder why people smoked. Now I wonder how anyone can give it up.

I sit on the deck and puff my brains out, one cigarette after another, until the whole pack is gone. I don't think about much while I inhale, just about how I might actually quit and if I really could become a millionaire based on my experience. I'm sure I could write a book about it. Or at least a blog. People would want to hear all about how I did it. Quitting really could make me millions.

But then again, what's millions compared to this rush?

I bury the cigarettes in the backyard like a dog before my wife comes home. I know I'll be looking for them tonight.

Garbage Disposals, Wedding Rings, and Potato Kings

When Theodore Wistang's wedding ring slipped off his finger and went down the drain, into the garbage disposal no less, he knew he had to retrieve it. Even though it wasn't his fault—it just slipped off in the soapy water during the dish duty—it would still be his fault and cause an uproar not seen for hundreds of years. No doubt all war would break loose, especially if he said the horrible dishonest words, "It wasn't my fault."

Theodore closed his eyes and reached his hand slowly into the sink, praying the disposal wouldn't suddenly flick on and chop off his hand and swallow his body whole.

He got part of his wish. The thing didn't turn on, but the drain did suddenly expand and suck down his body whole.

Theodore held his breath as he traveled through the endless winding drain, past the slime and sludge and hairballs and things he couldn't ever recognize because they certainly came from the depths of hell and not from his world.

When he finally landed, he found himself in a world that made the inside of the drain seem like paradise.

Theodore was surrounded by everything he could ever imagine had gone down the garbage disposal, all hacked up but magically pieced back together and left all scarred and bandaged, thrown together and sewn up by some evil doctor whose knowledge of sewing was next to none.

Pork fat, egg shells, chicken bones, puddles of grease, carrots, watermelon rinds, and thousands of other disposed food particles surrounded him, chanting in some strange language that sounded almost like the whirring blades of a garbage disposal. He tried to decipher what they were saying, but their voices were too muffled. The stench of all the rotting food blasted through the air, blocking all his senses. Theodore scrambled to his feet, but he slipped on a pile of moldy apple sauce and found himself on the ground and face-to-face with the king of all the rotten garbage, the skin of a Yukon gold potato. It didn't seem all that menacing, but the thing gave off the air of authority. Theodore shat himself and vomited right on the potato's crown.

"Are you kidding me?" the potato shouted.

Theodore closed his eyes and flinched, fearing the wrath of the great potato and its army.

"Hey, I'm talking to you," the potato said.

"What is this place?" Theodore managed to mumble.

"Hmm, let's see, it's at the bottom of your drain, there's a lot of rotten food leftovers. What do you think it is? It's fucking Disneyland," the potato said.

The rotting food surrounding the potato laughed. The laugh was tinny and cold and sent shivers up and down Theodore.

"I just want my ring," Theodore said once the shivers had ceased.

"And I just want my filling back," the potato skin said. Again the food particles laughed.

Theodore shook his head and gathered himself. He wasn't about to be afraid of the unwanted leftovers of a potato.

"Give me my ring now!" he shouted at the potato.

"Give me my filling now!" the potato shouted right back before hurling some stray sour cream in Theodore's left eye.

When Theodore had finished wiping the sour cream away, he noticed the army of food particles had closed in even tighter around him.

"Here's how this is going to work," the potato said. "You want your ring, and I want my filling. And I also want to get rid of most of this smelly junk." A flap of the potato skin swept over the expanse of garbage. "You're gonna help me get what I want, and then I'll help you get what you want."

"But how am I supposed—"

"Don't be so dense," the potato said. "You know what you're gonna do with all this junk."

Theodore's realization made him vomit again, but this time he missed the potato.

The potato smacked him across the face. "Get over yourself," it said.

Theodore shook his head and watched the trail of vomit-spit drip from his lips. He told himself to stay calm, that it was just a potato and that he could overcome this. His wife's reaction to the loss of the ring would be far worse. A rotting potato he could deal with.

Theodore stood and told the potato he would happily comply with the demands.

"Very well," said the potato, "wise choice. You may start with the meat scraps and fat."

Theodore looked at the mob of meat scraps and fat as it started to back away in fear. He wondered why they didn't just overthrow the potato right then and there. After all, how hard could it be to defeat the skin of a potato?

Theodore looked the potato right in the eyes and said, "If it's okay with you, I'd like to retrieve your stuffing before I take on this pile of waste. You see, I just ate not too long ago, so I don't think I have the appetite for it right now. But after my journey to recover your filling, I'll be quite hungry."

The potato returned Theodore's gaze and nodded in agreement. "You have two hours to return with my filling," the potato said, "or your ring is gone forever."

Theodore agreed to the terms and offered his hand to the potato. The potato didn't return the offer but instead directed a bread butt to assist Theodore in his return to the over world. "And make sure he doesn't try anything funny," the potato added quietly, just loud enough for Theodore to hear.

The bread butt showed Theodore the way back up the drain and through the garbage disposal. Theodore wondered what would happen if someone activated the switch while they were traveling through the metal blades, but luckily he didn't find out.

"No funny business," the bread butt said right before they emerged from the sink. Theodore was about to reply when he realized the bread butt had transformed back into just an inanimate bread butt. It wouldn't've been able to hear him no matter how loud he spoke.

Back in the comfort of his kitchen, the rank smell of mold and decaying food remained in Theodore's nose, as did the shit in his pants. He felt damp all over. For fear of being discovered by a family member, Theodore rushed to the pantry for a potato. He grabbed the first one he could find in the bag while he tried to devise a plan. The potato was smooth and hard, but it wasn't a Yukon gold. "That old potato skin will never notice," Theodore said aloud.

Grasping the potato tight in his hand, Theodore rushed to a drawer and pulled out a peeler. He went to work on the potato, not bothering to guide the skin into the sink. There was no point in sending anything else to that horrid world below. He didn't imagine he'd ever use the disposal again.

When the potato was fully peeled, Theodore hurried to the fridge and pulled out a half-eaten tub of sour cream. He slipped the tub into this pocket and then rushed to the sink. The bread butt was still sitting there soaking up the residual soapy water from Theodore's dish duty.

Theodore looked into the depths of the drain and wondered if he was just supposed to jump in or if there was some trick to it. Just to be safe, he pushed the bread down into the drain first and then called out to it.

"How do I go back down?" he said.

"The same way you did before," the bread responded, its muffled voice echoing through the hollows of the pipes.

Theodore slowly reached his empty hand into the drain once again, hoping the disposal wouldn't come to life. It didn't, but the drain once again opened and sucked his body down. The bread butt clung to his shirt and asked if he had the potato.

"Yeah, I've got it," Theodore replied as they accelerated much faster than the gravitational pull through the sludgy pipe.

Theodore and the bread butt landed in a pile of chicken parts and were immediately greeted by the potato.

"You have my filling?" the potato asked.

"It's right here," Theodore said, holding up the skinned potato.

The Yukon skin crawled closer to Theodore to inspect the filling with his many eyes.

"Not so fast," said Theodore. "I need to see that my ring is safe before I give you this."

"I don't make deals," the skin replied. "Let me inspect the merchandise."

"No deal," Theodore said.

"Then no ring," the skin said.

"I can buy a new ring. Where are you going to get new filling if not from me?"

The skin hesitated and stroked itself in thought. "I'm a patient potato," it said after several strokes. "I can wait. Eventually you'll send one down the drain."

"I don't think so," said Theodore. "I'm not using the disposal anymore. The only thing that's coming down is water, and soon you'll be flooded away. Now where's the ring?"

The potato skin lifted a flap of itself and showed a shiny metal band that he covered just as soon as Theodore could recognize the gleam.

"Happy?" the skin asked.

"Very much so," Theodore said. He handed the potato filling over to the skin. The skin breathed in and inhaled the scent of the uncooked potato body.

"Hmmm," it said. "I'm not so sure about this."

"It's the best you're going to get," Theodore replied before grabbing the folds of skin and pulling them together over the potato body.

The Yukon gold skin felt the body of the potato and smiled. It was good to be whole again. In its moment of contentment, Theodore struck with his great plan. Pulling out the tub of sour cream, he coated the potato in the white substance and then scooped it up and took a bite. The Yukon gold screamed as Theodore ripped through its newly restored flesh. Theodore shuddered and grimaced as the slimy skin and uncooked body clogged his throat. He swallowed hard, sending the potato down into his organs, and then went in for another bite.

"Attack him!" the diminishing potato shouted with his remaining strength. The bread butt led the charge, but most of the food did not follow. Instead, they cheered the defeat of their mighty dictator. Theodore fought off the bread butt as he continued to devour hunks of the potato. The bread butt was relentless in its attack, but Theodore prevailed as he grabbed and crumbled the soggy, moldy slice.

With just one bite of potato to go, Theodore reached for his ring and slid it on his finger. Then he tossed the remaining piece of potato into the cheering crowd of food waste. He leapt into the pipe and soared away before the army of waste could finish the assault on the potato.

When Theodore emerged from the sink smelling of shit and mildew, his wife was standing in the kitchen pulling a snack from the pantry. She turned at the thud of his body slapping against the tile.

"What the hell?" she cried out at the sight of her filthy drenched husband on the floor. "Where did you come from?"

"Just doing the damn dishes and taking out the trash," Theodore said.

"Take a shower when you're done," she said. "You smell awful." She looked at him and then at the floor. "Take care of that potato skin, too," she added.

He scooped it into his hands and walked to the trashcan.

"Don't put it in there you slob," she said. "Put it in the disposal. That's why we have the damn thing."

Theodore didn't bother arguing. He figured he could take another potato any day if he had to. He tossed the skin into the sink and flipped the switch. The disposal devoured the potato and it disappeared, hopefully forever. When Theodore turned off the disposal, he swore he heard a little cheer emerge from the depths of the earth. The tinny echo bounced around the sink and he wondered if his wife had heard it.

"Are we having potatoes for dinner?" she asked from the other side of the kitchen.

Theodore vomited in the sink at the thought of ever eating another potato. Then he sent that down the disposal as well. This time he didn't hear any cheering.

Getting the Meat

My wife and I wanted meatloaf, but we didn't have any meat ready. Shelly thought she could scrounge something up from the garage where we keep the big industrial freezer she insisted on getting because her sister had one. I was left cutting onions and measuring ingredients while she went to find the meat.

After ten minutes of chopping and pouring, I realized she hadn't returned. I put down my measuring cups and went to the garage to see what was taking so long. There she was hacking the shit out of a carcass, blood erupting all over her face and torso. She had my best hacksaw in her left hand and our hedge clippers in her right. I'd never seen such aggression.

"What the hell are you doing?"

Her lips curled into a smile, her pearly whites speckled bright red. She looked sexy.

"I'm getting the damn meat ready." She assaulted the body with the hedge clippers.

"What is that?"

"It's meat. I already told you that." The sawing of flesh and crunching of bone and tendon almost drowned out her words.

"What *kind* of meat?"

"What the hell's it matter?" She tugged with all her might. "Did you cut all the onions?" She set down the hacksaw and hedge clippers and used my heavy duty wood chisel to scrape the meat off the bones into a big cleaning bucket.

"Yeah, I just finished." I watched her boobs gyrate and her little arm muscles ripple.

"Great. Go get the food processor."

I ran inside, the fastest I'd moved in months, a young servant eagerly obeying his master.

When I got back into the garage, she yanked the processor from my hand and loaded it with the flesh. It was dark and thick, swirled with shades of tan and red.

"Take this out," she said, nodding to a stuffed garbage bag. "Take it out the backdoor." She switched on the food processor. The grinding was horrible, a cacophony of whirring and shrieking and clashing.

I lugged the trash outside. It easily weighed seventy pounds. Thank goodness for those extra heavy duty bags guaranteed not to rip. You know the ones. They have the commercial where a piano falls from the sky and lands in the bag and nothing breaks.

I tossed the bag into our trash bucket and it tore open. A couple of clean bones fell out. I picked one up and examined it like I was holding a rare archaeological find. I tried to figure out what type of animal yielded such bones, but I gave up and tossed it in the trash.

I picked up the torn bag and a few more bones slipped out, along with a pair of blood-stained jeans. I checked the tag, a size forty-four waist. Not ours. I tossed them into the trashcan and emptied the bag onto the grass. Among the pile of bones I found a green t-shirt, a pair of socks, and some tennis shoes. A belt and wallet came out last. I checked the wallet, but it was empty. I scooped up everything and tossed it into the bin, closed the lid and went inside.

"What took so long?"

"The bag broke."

"Shit. Those bags aren't supposed to break."

"I guess we should sue for false advertising."

She switched on the grinder and I watched the meat shred to itty pieces. "Last batch," she yelled.

On the floor I noticed over a dozen gallon-storage bags full of ground meat, zipped up to keep the blood from seeping out.

"Where the hell did you get all this meat?"

"At the store."

"How much did it cost?"

"I got a good deal." She laughed. "It was to die for."

Terrified and horny, I didn't want to get on her bad side, so I laughed with her.

"Should I get ready to cook the loaf?"

"Yup. Here's some meat." She tossed me a handful of ground flesh. In the kitchen, I slapped the clump of meat into a smooth loaf with my bare hands while working in the chopped onions, bread crumbs, and other ingredients. Satisfied with my work, I plopped the loaf into a pan and placed it in the oven. I wanted to go back in the garage and see Shelly at work, but I knew it was best to clean up first.

The doorbell rang while I was washing a bowl. I dried the bowl on my way to the door. My neighbor's wife, Janice, stood on the porch wearing a pencil skirt and a tight eggshell blouse that showed off her sizeable tits.

"What's up?" I asked.

I looked up from the bowl and noticed she'd been crying.

"Have you seen Darrel?"

I could tell she was trying not to sob and I felt a bit foolish when I realized I was still toweling off the bowl. "I saw him leave for work today."

"Who's at the door?" Shelly called.

"It's Janice."

"Invite her in for some meat."

"Want some meat loaf?" I asked.

"I need to find my husband."

She seemed preoccupied as though she were worried something terrible had happened. Knowing Darrel, I figured he was fornicating in a cheap motel. That was Darrel's style. He wouldn't spring for a nice place.

"Do you have any idea where he might be?"

"Probably stuck in traffic, that's all."

"I've called four times and he hasn't answered once. Something's wrong. We're supposed to go out tonight, and he's over two hours late."

I looked at my watch and saw it was after seven. Shelly had been chopping meat for almost two hours now.

"I'm sure he'll turn up. You know Darrel." I laughed at this, not really sure what I meant. "You must be hungry though. Come have some meat loaf. Then we can go look for Darrel together." I wasn't sure why I said that either, but some ideas rushed through my head while I thought about running around town with Janice looking for her fornicating husband. It was almost as hot as my wife covered in blood hacking the shit out of some carcass. I know it sounds weird, but I'm not a fetish guy or anything. I've never done anything kinky. It was just hot though.

"I guess I can do that." She looked distant and unsure. Her eyes were sunken and I wasn't sure she could even see out of them. "Let me go change first."

I wasn't happy about that. No doubt she'd come back looking less sexy.

Shelly was in the kitchen getting a drink of water. With blood stains all over her sweaty body, she looked like one of those buff chicks in a workout video, all tan and glistening, but it was like a horror workout video where she'd just finished a workout that involved killing people. A murder workout. Now that's a fitness craze I could see catching on.

"Is Janice coming over?"

"Yup, she's coming. Had to change first. Want to get cleaned up?" I gave her a wink.

"And her husband?" She threw me a devilish smile.

"Oh yeah. Funny story. She can't find him and he won't return her calls. He's probably with some number from the office."

"Or maybe he's stuffed in a trashcan somewhere."

Her laugh doubled mine, her sweat-and-blood-covered body rippling with each chuckle. I just wanted to get her in the shower.

"C'mon, let's get cleaned up."

"But there's no time for messing around. We need to get our feast ready. We can't just serve meatloaf. That would be barbaric."

She started laughing again, so I laughed too, picturing Janice sitting there, probably in jeans and a sweatshirt, eating nothing but meatloaf.

"Can you imagine Janice just eating meatloaf?"

She doubled over at the image. "Maybe she'll figure out where her husband is then."

I laughed too, not really sure what was so funny about that. Truth is I felt a little bad for Janice. She had no idea her husband was such a sleaze ball. I couldn't imagine what it must be like to be married to someone who could do such terrible things.

While she showered, I cut some vegetables and heated a few baked potatoes in the microwave. I opened a bottle of wine, a nice cabernet, and then set the table for three. It was odd seeing three place settings.

My wife was still in the shower when Janice came back. She was wearing jeans and a sweatshirt, just as I had predicted. I wondered what her panties looked like.

I offered her a glass of wine. "Did Darrel come home yet?"

She shook her head. "No, Darrel's still not back, and he still isn't answering his phone."

I poured a full glass for myself. "That's so bizarre. Want me to call?"

She sighed. "If you want."

I pulled out my phone and dialed. My wife came downstairs in a tank top with her hair still wet. A cell phone started ringing in the garage.

"Honey, I think your phone is ringing," I said, covering up the mouthpiece.

"That's funny," Janice said. "You have the same ring tone as Darrel."

Shelly shook her head. "That's not mine."

Janice bolted for the garage and returned with her husband's phone.

"What the hell is Darrel's phone doing in your garage?"

Shelly shrugged. "Honey, why don't you get out the meatloaf."

I did as I was told, wondering if maybe Darrel had left his phone in there last night when we drank a few beers and stared at the car.

Shelly opened a cabinet and pulled out the still-bloodied hacksaw. I stood frozen in the kitchen holding the meatloaf.

"You can toss that out," she said. "Change in the menu."

She sliced into Janice's face with the hacksaw. Blood squirted in all directions.

The meatloaf slipped out of my shaking hands. "What the hell are you doing?"

She didn't seem to hear as she ripped the hacksaw right through Janice's breasts. She tossed one to me. "I've seen you eye these boobs before. Enjoy the feast."

My eyes widened as I observed the brutal killer my wife had become. She clutched the hacksaw like it was a prized possession. She was panting and had a deranged look on her face. I looked at the bloody body and the meatloaf on the floor and it all started to make sense. Except I had no idea why my wife had murdered our neighbors.

"So are you just going to stare, or are you going to screw me?"

I didn't bother to ask questions. We'd never screwed so hard in our entire marriage. The sex was the best I'd ever had. And the new meatloaf was as delicious. It only took a bite to realize why she'd done it. It was the best meal of my life. Now we have a freezer filled with packages of ground up meat. That stupid freezer finally paid off.

Skydivers and Pornographers

Marcus had to redo the big scene for *Going Down Without a Chute*. His costar passed out in midair before he'd even taken off his pants. Jana fumed when she heard the news.

"It's just skydiving," he said.

"Is it even possible?"

He rubbed her gently, making her quiver like a reed in a torrent. "Of course it's possible. I just need you there. You're my inspiration." She succumbed to his touch, her body collapsing on the couch.

"I'll be there," she sighed. For a moment she felt like one of his costars, but then she remembered it was just a suede couch. He was off her before it was over anyway, his belt barely buckled as he told her to get in the car or they'd be late.

Marcus was a pioneer, the innovator of the genre. First there was the mountain climbing scene. He didn't even use gear, although his costar wore a harness. Then he rode a horse and a woman to victory in an actual horserace. Then cageless scuba diving with sharks. There was the gator-filled swamp scene, the wall rappel, the jousting match. And of course there was the scene that had made him the most famous of all, the flaming bed of nails.

He'd survived it all, to rave reviews, and the women, oh the women, how they came and came and came. Just once Jana wished he could do to her what he did to them, but she was too afraid. She would try to support him though, even as he jumped out of a plane and somehow found the dexterity to penetrate a strange woman. Only the woman would wear a parachute, so he couldn't remove himself from her until they reached the ground.

When they arrived, Marcus gave her a rough kiss on the cheek and thanked her for coming. She wished him good luck and returned his kiss.

Jana watched as Marcus jumped from the plane and shed his clothes. He stripped the woman and found a way to keep himself inside her as they pierced the delicate clouds. The parachute didn't even tangle when he turned her

NATHANIEL TOWER | **69**

around. Jana could hear the woman moaning thousands of feet above the ground. It gave her a strange twinge of excitement.

When Marcus landed and dismounted, Jana gave him a hug and said she was proud of him. "Can we give it a try?" she cooed in his ear.

"I don't mix work and pleasure," he said. "Besides, I need to do another take with Amber. I made her moan too soon."

Marcus went off to the trailer. Jana, fuming again, sneaked off to the prop box. She didn't bother to wish Marcus good luck.

Grounded, Jana watched her husband penetrate the sky and the woman again. This time the chute didn't open. Marcus and Amber fell faster and faster, Marcus thrusting all the way, Amber howling to the ground, Jana getting in the car before it was over.

Doctor Worthington's Lump

Doctor Harvey Worthington had been lying awake for almost fifteen minutes. Since there was nothing better to do, he performed a self exam. He used a simple pinch and roll, a technique he found favorable. The brief joy he received was quickly overshadowed by the discovery of an extraneous bump. It felt like a pea had lodged itself in his scrotum, but he couldn't remember eating any peas.

As soon as his fingers discovered the protuberance, he sat up, startling his wife Carol.

"What's wrong?" she cooed.

"I have cancer," the doctor replied.

"What do you mean?" Her voice showed both her concern and her desire for more rest.

"There's a lump, down in my testicles. I have cancer."

"You can't possibly know that," she tried to reassure while stifling a ferocious yawn that came out anyway.

"Carol, honey, I think I know when I have cancer. After all, I am a doctor," he added matter-of-factly.

Carol rolled her eyes. Harvey was a doctor, something he pointed out to everyone he met. He was a doctor of philosophy, which he claimed was the truest of sciences.

"I'm sure it will be okay," she muffled into her pillow.

"No, darling, it won't be. I'm only giving myself two years, tops."

Just as he spoke, the alarm began its annoying buzz, prompting him to feel his testicles again. This time, the lump felt more like a golf ball.

"It's growing!" he cried, flinging off the sheets and revealing his naked body. He pulled his body up to his knees, his bulging sack hanging between his legs. "Look at this lump," he shouted while pointing to the mass.

Carol glanced and said, "It looks fine to me."

"Fine? It looks like I have three balls!"

She didn't respond.

"How can you even think about sleeping at a time like this?"

"Because I'm tired."

"I can't believe you're ignoring my impending death," he said. He looked down again at the appendages between his legs. The lump was now the size of a tennis ball. "It's growing by the second! It's an exponential growth curve!"

"I'm so impressed by your mathematical abilities," Carol said.

"Would you just look at the damn thing? I might be dead before the hour is over and all you can think about is a few extra minutes of sleep."

Carol sat up again. "Testicular cancer is highly treatable. Over ninety-five percent of men are fully cured within a year. Very rarely is it fatal."

"I can't believe you aren't taking this more seriously."

Carol stared at his naked body and became playful. "Would you like me to examine it for you?" she said as she mounted him like a bronco.

"How can you even think about sex?" He gave her a forceful shove and reached for his robe, covering his naked body before Carol could see that his lump had grown as big as a grapefruit.

"Calm down, baby. You're going to be fine. We'll make a doctor's appointment."

"For heaven's sake, dear. Why must you insist on belittling my own education?"

"Darling," she said, "why must you insist that *you* are a doctor? You don't know cancer. If you think you're dying, you need to see a real doctor. A *medical* doctor."

"Great. I'm dying *and* my wife thinks that I'm good for nothing." Doctor Worthington marched toward the bedroom door.

"Where are you going?"

"I'm going to church. I need to start working on saving my soul."

"You're ridiculous," she uttered before he completed his exodus.

On his way out of the bedroom Doctor Worthington took a glance at the now cantaloupe-sized lump and fell to the ground. The crash rattled the windows.

Doctor Worthington tried to cover the lump, but the robe wouldn't quite fit. The bedroom door pulled open and out came Carol.

"What are you doing on the floor?"

"Take me to the emergency room," the embarrassed doctor said.

"Are you hurt?"

"I have a watermelon growing out of my ballsack and I can't stay on my feet. Go start the car."

"Honey, don't you think you're exaggerating slightly? Other than looking a bit like a buffoon, you look fine."

The doctor didn't understand how his wife could be so cavalier.

"Just get the damn car running before we won't fit inside anymore."

"Fine," she said as she went back in the bedroom to dress.

Doctor Worthington pulled himself to his feet. He held the lump between his legs while leaning on the banister. The doctor descended the stairs, wincing with each step. A few minutes later, his wife passed him.

"Aren't you going to put something else on?"

"This is fine. They're just going to make me get naked anyway. Look, now. It's as big as a chair."

Carol shook her head and left him behind. A few minutes later, he flopped down in the backseat of the car, carefully dragging his furniture-sized scrotum behind him.

"What the hell are you doing back there?" Carol asked.

"I don't think I'll fit in the front," he moaned.

Carol drove him to the hospital, hitting several bumps along the way.

During the car ride, the lump grew so big that it got stuck on the way out of the car. It barely fit through the doublewide automatic doors to the ER, scraping on the cold metal edges as he entered.

Doctor Worthington was greeted with a stack of forms. The receptionist asked him what he felt on the pain scale. The doctor was disgusted.

"Seriously? Look at this lump." He opened his robe and showed his naked body to the nurse.

"Sir, please cover yourself up and answer our questions."

While trying to close the robe the best he could, the doctor muttered, "It doesn't really hurt so much as it is just inconvenient." Now that he thought about it, he wondered why it didn't hurt, especially given how much it stretched out the soft tissues of his scrotum and forced so much extra weight to tug at his testicles.

"Okay, Mr. Worthington, have a seat."

"It's Doctor," he corrected.

"Yes, a doctor will be with you shortly."

He would've argued, but he really needed to find a good seat to rest himself.

"This is so embarrassing," his wife muttered, her hands hiding her face.

"Ha. *You're* embarrassed? What about me?" He found an open row of seats to rest his lump. He begrudgingly picked up a copy of *People Magazine* because *The Economist* was too far away to drag his body.

Doctor Worthington flipped through the magazine four times, stopping to read a few captions here and there. As he opened the cover a fifth time, his name was finally called.

"Mr. Harvey Worthington," a blonde nurse said, "the doctor will see you now."

He thought about making a joke about seeing himself, but he wasn't really in the mood.

He tried to stand, but the weight of the now horse-sized lump prevented him from moving.

"Could I get a wheelchair?" he asked.

"Okay," the nurse said with mild uncertainty. She looked at Carol who shrugged in return. Carol asked Harvey if she wanted him to come with him to the room. He told her it was best she not. She shrugged and picked up a magazine.

The nurse returned a moment later with a wheelchair.

"Do you have any of those doublewide ones?" Harvey wondered.

"Let's see if this one works for you first," the nurse said.

Harvey sat down reluctantly, his lump spilling off the chair and dragging on the floor as the nurse pushed him to the room. He was impressed by her ability to push him so easily.

"Here you go, Mr. Worthington," she said when they arrived at the room. She squeezed him and the lump through the doorframe. "The doctor will be here shortly."

He already is, thought Harvey. The nurse handed him a gown and left. He saw no point in putting it on.

The room was so small that Harvey immediately began to feel claustrophobic. He felt like he was being swallowed, and he knew the lump would burst through the walls at any moment.

Harvey waited for at least ten minutes. If the doctor didn't get there soon, either the room or Harvey would surely explode.

Just as the pressure of the lump squeezing against the walls became unbearable, the doctor burst through the door. Harvey's lump spilled into the hallway.

"So, Mr. Worthington, I hear you have a lump," the doctor said while staring at a chart.

"Yup."

"I'm sorry to hear that. I'm Dr. Andrews. Would you please take off your robe so I may have a look?"

Harvey looked at him blankly.

"Don't be shy, Mr. Worthington," Dr. Andrews said, "I've seen it all."

Harvey dropped his robe and stood naked. The doctor moved closer to inspect the lump, somehow avoiding the sack as he worked.

"Yes, yes, I see," Dr. Andrews muttered as he fondled Harvey's lump.

"Well, what do you see?" Harvey asked.

Dr. Andrews took off his glove. The glove snapped as it came off, and the doctor responded to the snap by saying, "You have a lump, but it's nothing out of the ordinary."

"Nothing out of the ordinary?" Harvey cried. "Are you kidding? It's taking over the hospital. Can't you cut it off?"

"I'm afraid that would do more damage than you'd probably like," the doctor said.

"Well, what is it?" Harvey wondered. By now, the lump had filled the hallway.

"It's called a varicocele. Some people refer to it as a bag of worms." Dr. Andrews scribbled something on the chart.

"That's it? A giant bag of worms is taking over my body? Are they eating me from the inside?" Harvey felt a bit faint.

"More than twenty percent of men have them. They don't serve any serious problems. You might experience a twinge of pain, and it's possible that it affects your fertility. The surgery is rather invasive and not recommended. I wouldn't worry about it at all," Dr. Andrews said. With those words, he stepped over the massive lump and disappeared into the hallway.

Harvey sat down in the wheelchair and wheeled himself back into the waiting area. He could feel patients and nurses staring at him as he looked for Carol.

"What're you doing, Harvey?" his wife cried.

"I'm leaving. These people are idiots here."

"Where's your robe?" she cried.

"What's the use? It won't fit over the lump."

"Let's get out of here before you get arrested," Carol said in a panic. She walked swiftly out of the hospital and to the car. The lump trailed behind. It was still in the waiting room when the couple was almost to the car, blocking the doorway and forcing several ambulances to wait.

Carol unlocked the car and got in. She didn't bother asking Harvey what the doctor said. Harvey wondered how he was going to get the lump inside. He wondered if he could just break it off by slamming the car door on it. As Carol started the car, Harvey got an idea. He grabbed the lump and started to roll it up like a hose. It became more and more compact until he could squeeze it into the backseat.

Carol ranted almost the whole way home about how embarrassed she was. Harvey tuned her out as he wondered how he would ever get into his pants again.

"What am I going to do?" Harvey moaned in the back.

"I don't know, but you'd better figure it out in the next few months," Carol replied.

"Why's that?" Harvey asked knowing he probably wouldn't be around that long.

"Well, honey, this may be a bit of a surprise, but we're pregnant!"

Harvey's eyes met Carol's briefly in the rearview. Then he looked back at the lump and the gray hairs surrounding it. For a brief moment, the lump seemed a little smaller as Harvey realized he had bigger problems on his hands.

The Most Beautiful Toes

Sherry Sandra Soutmore never once removed her toenail polish. The moment she saw any flaking or cracking, she simply covered the old coat with a new one. She preferred using shades of orange, but occasionally she mixed things up with a hot pink or bright red. She once tried to go clear, but even after applying seven layers of the clear polish, a vibrant orange somehow shone through.

Sherry only wore flip flops and open-toed high heels. If she wasn't wearing those, she was bare foot. She wanted everyone to see her lovely painted toes.

Sherry's toes were indeed beautiful. They weren't exceptionally long or short or stubby. She didn't have that odd second-toe-bigger-than-the-big-toe syndrome. Her big toe was the biggest, and the rest got proportionately smaller after that, all the way down to that adorable pinkie toe. That little toe could make men melt.

She couldn't have worn sneakers if she had tried. Although one layer of nail polish is untraceably thin, thousands of layers quickly add up. Since she began painting her toenails at age seven, she had been religious about applying a new layer at least every three days. By age thirty-six, Sherry's toes were obviously overwhelmed with paint.

One big advantage the thick nails gave Sherry was she didn't have to bend down very far to paint them. Most women had to awkwardly get down on the ground and reach and strain to get to the toes. Sherry just had to lean a little, even if she was standing up. This allowed her to paint her toes just about anywhere. She was never more proud of herself than when she first painted her toes while driving. That she made it home without an accident was just a bonus.

The only disadvantages to the thick layers of paint were trying to put on tapered pants or putting feet underneath a seat on an airplane. Otherwise, they were quite nice.

On the eve of her thirty-seventh birthday, Sherry's husband of fifteen years, Andrew Soutmore, decided he had had enough.

"Either the polish goes, or I go," he told Sherry. He wasn't talking about the dozens and dozens of containers of nail polish that cluttered the bathroom floor.

"And what do you propose I do about it?" Sherry said.

"I have plenty of turpentine in the garage. I can take care of this in a few hours."

Sherry looked down at her toes and then up at her husband. He was quite handsome, even at forty-one, and he was successful. He had always provided for her, and he even painted her toes for her a few times when she was pregnant with the twins. She couldn't let him go after all these years.

"Fine," she said, tears in her eyes. She wanted to say that if he really loved her then he would let her keep the polish, but she knew that he could come right back with if she really loved him then she would give it up. That could go on all day, so she decided just to agree to get rid of the polish. She could always start a new collection. That would be a lot easier than finding a new husband willing to put up with thousands of layers of nail polish. Her feet had also grown quite heavy as of late, and she had been hoping to shed a few pounds.

Andrew went to the garage and returned to the bedroom less than a minute later with a container of turpentine.

"Put your feet in the bathtub," he directed her.

She did as he said.

Andrew immediately began pouring turpentine on her toes. At first, the turpentine splashed off the thick layers and all over the tiled floor, but soon the layers started to wear away. Every few seconds, Andrew would stop pouring and start scrubbing at the toes with a bristle pad. Then he would continue pouring the turpentine on her feet. Unfortunately, Andrew ran out of turpentine long before Sherry ran out of toenails.

"Now what?" Sherry asked, upset that half her polish was gone and that the current layer was a mixture of thirteen shades of orange. "My toes look disgusting. It looks like an orange rainbow vomited all over them."

"I've never seen an orange rainbow," Andrew replied. He stood quietly for a moment scratching his chin. Sherry was beginning to feel exposed.

"I've got it," he finally said.

Andrew left the bedroom and returned a short time later with a power sander.

"We'll get that polish off yet."

He turned on the power sander and began working on Sherry's toes. Sherry winced in pain as the sandpaper vibrated hard across her toenails. Although it was still far from the actual skin of her toes, the vibrations seemed to tug at the nails in a way that made it feel like they were going to be torn from her feet.

"Honey, this really hurts," she said at the precise moment that a shard of polish caught Andrew in the eye. Somehow he maintained his grip on the sander and continued to carve away at her toes.

"Just a few more minutes," he spat out with his eyes closed.

Thousands of polish particles had clung to his hair, and Sherry laughed at his clownish appearance. She was glad to have the distraction.

"What are you laughing at?" he shouted over the sander's hum.

"You look like Bozo," she laughed.

"At least I didn't have twenty-five inches of toe nail polish on my feet." The words came out spitefully, and Sherry quickly ceased her laughing.

"Stop!" she shouted at her husband.

The power sander quivered to a halt.

"What the hell was that supposed to mean?" Sherry was fuming. Her cheeks were brighter than her toenails.

Andrew began stuttering. "Uh, I, um, I, I mean..."

"Cat got your tongue?" she said.

"No, your toenails cut it up too much," he managed to spit.

Sherry stood up, grabbed the power sander, and threw it against the window. The window cracked and the sander fell to the floor. She marched over to her toenail polish collection and grabbed the first color she could find.

"Don't act like I'm the only one in the wrong here," she yelled as she slathered fuchsia polish all over her toenails. She bent down uncomfortably to do it, her toes only about half the size of what they had been when her husband started his handiwork.

"Honey," her husband began with skillful articulateness, "I've put up with a lot because of these damn toenails. You know everyone talks about it. Do you know what people say about you? They all think you're crazy. And they think I'm crazy too."

"Nobody thinks I'm crazy," she argued, her toenails beginning to fill out again as she started working on her third bottle.

"Yes, they all do. And you know what? What you are doing is bad for our kids. You know what I found in Josh's room the other day?" Andrew was fuming now. As he spoke, the flakes of nail polish charged out of his hair and landed on the floor. Sherry eyed them enviously and wondered if she could reattach them to her toes.

"Cigarettes?" she asked, not really paying attention to what her husband was saying.

"No," he shouted. "This." He pulled a bottle of mango nail polish out of his pocket. "Our son has been painting his toenails."

"All boys experiment at some time," she shrugged, now on her fourth bottle.

"He's thirteen years old. He's too old to be applying nail polish." Andrew threw the bottle on the floor. It clattered, but it didn't break.

"You're overreacting to this," Sherry said as she reached for her fifth bottle. She was no longer applying the polish so much as she was just pouring it on to her feet.

"No, I'm not. I'm saying what I should've said fifteen years ago. And you're ruining our floor."

Sherry silently dumped another bottle of nail polish on her toenails. There was no pattern to her color selection now, and her feet were completely soaked in the polish. The odor was beginning to overwhelm the couple.

"I think you should stop," Andrew said as he began to sway from side to side.

"I can't stop now," she replied. "My toenails are uneven." She dumped another bottle on her feet.

Andrew turned to leave, but he slipped on a puddle of polish and landed with a thud on his back. A cloud of polish dust formed around him and then settled on top of his chest. His head rested right beside his wife's painted feet.

Sherry kept working on her toenails. She pulled a sponge out from underneath the sink and began spreading the polish around. Things were only looking more uneven.

"I'm running out of polish," she cried.

Her husband didn't respond.

"Go get some more polish for me," she said to him as she emptied the last bottle on her feet.

He still didn't respond.

She nudged him with her right foot. His body rocked and then settled. He gave no other response.

"I guess I'll just have to do it myself," she said in annoyance. She tried to stand, but she couldn't get enough traction. She would have to wait until all of the polish dried. The odor of the polish was becoming almost unbearable. She hadn't noticed it so much when she was busy painting, but now that she had nothing to do, the smell was all she could think about. She tried to open the window, but it was out of reach, as was the exhaust fan.

Sherry knew she was going to faint any moment. She prodded her husband with her feet, at first gently, and then she started kicking at his head as if he were a soccer ball. She continued this motion until her body gave out. Then she too lay motionlessly, her feet brightly decorated in every array of orange possible. Had anyone been looking through their bathroom window, the emanating light from the bright orange feet would have appeared in a way that would have put the Northern Lights to shame. Sherry Soutmore really did have the most beautiful toes in the world.

A Blade of Love, Part Two: Love's Sharp Blade

The summer's sun has long ago burnt out, and the crispness of autumn has left most lawns covered with leaves. But not Allan Thermoose's lawn. Every morning and evening, and sometimes even during his lunch break, he circles the lawn with a gentle leaf vacuum. The leaves vanish from his yard before they can even dry out.

Allan is tired of doing yard maintenance, but he has no choice. It's all he really has left in life. When he's not maintaining the yard or slaving away at work, he's standing in the window, staring at his wife while she lies with her new love. Sometimes it makes Allan visibly ill (not that she sees it) to watch the two of them together, his wife caressing the long skin of the erect blade that captured her heart. It's all the woman ever does anymore. Allan tries to think of a time when she caressed him such a way, but his mind is as empty as the gutters he cleans twice a day.

The blade is now fifteen inches tall. It's unsightly and has tarnished Allan's reputation around the neighborhood. He used to be admired for such meticulous lawn care. Now his neighbors snicker that he can't even control one single piece of grass. Not to mention his wife. None of their wives are in love with plants.

Allan's wife has taken to eating her meals outside, and she sleeps there every night as well. The cool weather hasn't driven her in, but they haven't gotten a good freeze yet. Allan wonders how she'll handle that, how she'll deal with the inevitable hardening of the earth and browning of the grass.

He thinks about acting, about charging out there and taking back his wife, but he knows that biding his time is his best bet. The blade of grass must die, and he will be there in her time of need.

Allan's tried to move on. He had a brief fling with the juniper in the backyard, and the bark of the elm tree gave him one heck of a weekend, but nothing has lasted. He hasn't let it last. Those things just don't compare to his wife, or to her blade of grass.

Twice now she's caught him attempting to kill it. The first time was with weed killer. Then she saw him ready to release the beetles. She hasn't had to physically intervene yet. She just has to give him the look, that little pout she used to give him back when she wanted him to do things for her other than lawn care. But it's not the same look. There's just something a bit off about the way she does it now. He can't quite pinpoint it, but it's just not the same.

On a Tuesday, the frost comes. His wife sleeps outside *on top of* the blade. Allan tells himself she's just doing that to keep it warm, but he can't help but feel there's something else going on. He watches all night, and he swears she thrusts a few times. And in the morning, he finds her body all limp and exhausted, and somehow she's covered in sweat despite the freezing temperature.

"What were you doing out there?" he asks when she steps inside for her morning coffee. He stopped asking this question weeks ago, but now he has reason to ask it again.

"Just keeping him warm," she says. She's started calling it a him. Pretty soon she'll name the thing.

It's just grass! he wants to scream, but he can't scream. Not at her. Instead he hands her a cup of the coffee he brewed moments before she came inside. She takes a sip and thanks him. He waits for a kiss, but she doesn't give him one. He can't recall the last time her lips even so much as brushed his cheek.

"What are you going to do today?" he asks before taking his own sip.

"I'm teaching Gordon to play checkers," she says after another sip.

So she's done it. She's gone and named a piece of grass. She's truly lost her mind.

"Sounds fun." Allan pauses. "Can I play the winner?" He regrets asking almost immediately, but she surprises him and tells him that sounds nice.

He thinks he's won something, but then she snaps, "So you're finally making an effort."

Allan can't believe that he's somehow the bad guy in this situation. After all he's done. The hundreds of hours he's spent helping Gordon thrive! Doesn't this woman appreciate anything?

"You know, Gordon's been asking for weeks when you are going to play with him. He's been awfully hurt by the way you've treated him with the cold shoulder." She starts whispering. "And he thinks you're trying to kill him."

"Gordon is just a blade of grass!" he finally lets out. The release feels good until her hand comes across his face.

"How dare you!" she shouts as she winds up for a second slap. Her palm strikes him again, this time on the ear. His ear thumps like a bass drum and keeps thumping.

"That's it!"

Allan storms off to the garage and grabs everything with the slightest sense of sharpness. An axe, hedge clippers, an ice chisel, hacksaw, jigsaw, circular saw, handsaw, a saw he can't name, a large knife that looks like something you'd take to the rainforest. A chainsaw. Piling it all in a wheelbarrow, Allan throws open the garage and drags his tools to meet Gordon face to face. Of course his wife is already there, sitting like a crab to block Gordon from every direction without crushing him.

"Where's that damn blade!" he shouts at her as he spills the contents of the wheelbarrow unto the recently buzzed lawn.

"Stay away from Gordon!" his wife screams in a panic as her body recoils and bends Gordon's delicate body.

"I told you he was trying to kill me," Allan thinks he hears the grass say, but it might be the wind or the clanging of the sharp tools or his crazed mind. One can only take so much ridiculousness before going crazy.

Allan glares at his wife before reaching for the first tool he can find. It's the hacksaw.

"Get out of my way," he shouts as he wields it above his head. A neighbor passing by with his dog asks if everything is okay. Allan looks back just as the dog relieves itself on a patch of Allan's manicured lawn.

"You better clean that shit up," he yells, waving the hacksaw at the man and dog.

The man and his dog run away. Allan throws the hacksaw with the precision of an archer, and its jagged teeth pierce the pile of shit.

Unarmed, Allan turns and reaches for another weapon, but his wife has beaten him to the punch. She's holding the chainsaw inches from his neck, swearing she'll pull the cord and slice his head clean off if he dares to move closer to Gordon.

"You'll do no such thing," he tells her and follows it with, "You don't even know how to operate that thing."

She pulls the cord, the blade starts to engage, but the machine putters and whirs and coughs and stops. Allan hasn't gassed the device in quite some time.

Before she can pull the cord again, Allan dives to the pile of sharp instruments and selects, not by choice, the first thing his hand can grab. It's the hedge clippers. The blades are very sharp; Allan has been spending at least thirty minutes a week prepping them for this moment, a moment he thought would never come but has dreamed about nevertheless.

Just as Allan begins to stand, he feels the base of the chainsaw come down on his back. For a moment he is paralyzed, and his body drops like cement to the turf. The shock wears off after a second, and Allan realizes his wife is not trying to deliver a fatal blow. The woman could've used the blade, but she spared him. This is just about protection for her.

Before he can get too sentimental about it, his wife brings the chainsaw down on his left foot. This time she does use the blade. It lacerates through his ragged sweatpants and pierces the flesh of his ankle.

Allan's body rolls as the pain radiates up his leg. Everything he just thought is erased. His wife's out for blood. This is about more than just Gordon or any blade of grass. This is about his inadequacies as a husband. He's paid more attention to the lawn than he has to her, and now she's paying him back. The fling with Gordon isn't real. It's just an evil revenge ploy. "Good show," he says aloud, congratulating his wife on such a brilliant display of vengeance. "You've taught me a lesson. I'll be a better husband from now on. I will give you the attention you deserve." He continues to roll back and forth during his speech, never once glancing at her. Finally, when his speech is over and the pain has subsided, the pain he now knows was only in his heart and not in his leg, he ceases the rolling and looks up at his wife. She's standing over him, holding the chainsaw in both hands, a terrified look sunken deep in her eyes. The chainsaw slips out of her fragile hands. She's no chainsaw wielding maniac. She's just the wife of Allan Thermoose, and she loves the man very much.

Allan sees the love pour out of her eyes. She drops her body on top of his, and the two commence a duet of rolling in the grass. The husband and wife plant kisses all over each other, and their kisses fertilize the roots of their once passionate love. Allan tears off her gown just as she rips Allan's shirt. It's a scene from a romance novel, the passion unequaled by anything the earth has ever seen. The lawn, that perfectly manicured lawn, is their lush bedroom. The grass conforms to the curves of their thrusting bodies and provides more comfort than the greatest mattress man has yet to create. Their bodies become part of the lawn, and the grass suddenly seems to form around their planted bodies. The passersby don't even notice their love-making, which is so passionate now that any onlooker would certainly think they were killing each other. Their eyes are so tightly shut that *they* can't even recognize what it is they are doing. What's happening between them is something no human beings have ever seen before, not even with the most powerful microscope they've created. Their backs arch, their bodies thrust, their loins explode, all in unison, and it's all done motionlessly and noiselessly.

Hours later, the couple is spent. Their bodies, covered in grass, convulse sporadically through no awareness of their own. The sun has set and risen on their bodies, which still haven't moved of their own accord. Slowly, energy returns and their bodies emerge from the soil and shake off the grass.

Finally, the lovers open their eyes to see each other. The love embrace of their eyes lasts only a minute before they see Gordon towering over them, axe raised high. Then they become part of the earth once more.

A Cloning Affair

The day his wife left, Arnold Liggins found a huge clump of hair in the drain. It was his Claire's hair. Unmistakably hers. There might've been a little of his mixed in, but he couldn't see it if there was.

Arnold found the hair after she left. He didn't see it coming. She just packed the bags and left without offering much explanation. He didn't think it had anything to do with the drainage problem they were having in the bathtub. She had complained about it once or twice, but he'd never seen at as an urgent issue. When he took that first shower after her departure, he decided he was sick of standing in a puddle of soapy water. So he pulled out that ball of hair, pinching it between his thumb and forefinger. He pulled it out with vengeance.

The hair was yellow as the sun, at least when it was on her head. But in the tangled ball of dripping hair, it looked more brownish than he remembered. Had he forgotten her already? It'd only been a few hours.

Standing there naked, his body dripping water at the same rate as the hair, he felt alone for the first time in his life. He thought in that moment about making a deal with God or the devil to transform this lump of hair into his wife. She wouldn't be the same wife. Since he was creating her, there were more than a few things he would change, but she would more or less be the same woman, at least close enough that no one would notice he'd gotten a new wife. Unfortunately it occurred to him quickly that neither the God nor the devil would likely make a deal with him, especially given that he didn't really believe in either of them.

Realizing these hairs were the only connection he had to his wife at the moment, he fondled them for but a moment longer, staring at the details of each intertwined strand.

After this short inspection of the fibers, he tossed the clump in the trashcan. He didn't see much use for a bunch of hair. He went about his business, but later that night he found the hair had made its way into bed with him.

"What the hell?" he said to the hair. He didn't intend for it to be a question the hair would answer. And the hair didn't answer. It just remained a motionless, silent clump of tangled thread lying on the pillow next to his, just inches from his face.

He decided to take a whiff to see if it smelled like his wife. It did in a strange way—mostly because of the rosemary hints from the shampoo—but at the same time it smelled like rust and mildew, scents he had never noticed on his wife. Then again, his wife hadn't spent weeks in the drain.

"Would you mind scooting over?" he told the hair. He didn't think it would listen, but he felt lonely enough to talk to it. He wasn't much in the mood to be so close to something that smelled so foul and yet reminded him of his wife.

When the hairball actually started scooting away, Arnold assumed that this was nothing more than a dream, which in turn made him think that maybe his wife hadn't left at all. He chuckled to himself and decided he couldn't wait to wake up and tell his wife about the silly dream he'd had. She would laugh and hug him tightly and tell him that she would never leave him and then they would make love in positions they had never made love in before.

Although he was excited about the prospects of waking up and being intimate with his wife, he didn't want to rush it. This was too interesting, he thought, and would make a great story.

As Arnold thought about what a great story this would make and stared at the clump of hair, it occurred to him that this story was becoming a bit anticlimactic. The hair wasn't doing anything. He had to take some action.

Arnold started thinking of a film he'd once seen with one of those pretty-boy actors like Pitt or Clooney or Cage or maybe even Keanu Reeves. In the movie the pretty-boy actor cloned his wife or dog or sister or someone using some hair or bone or blood or sweat. The details weren't really important, but what was important was that if one of those actors could do such a thing then surely he could do it as well. After all, he must've been at least as smart as one of them.

So Arnold set to work cloning his wife from the clump of hair. He would make her the way he wanted her, changing some subtle things about her butt and face and personality, but she would mostly be the same woman he had married several years before.

It took several hours and a lot of improvising, but when Arnold stepped back to take a look at his finished product, he found himself smiling in a way he hadn't smiled before. He named his new wife Clara, figuring it was close enough to Claire that no one would notice the difference, yet it was different enough that he wouldn't be confused if Claire ever did return.

"So, are you just going to stand there, or are you going to take me out?" he heard Clara say after a few minutes of staring at the almost perfectly sculpted woman in front of him. Since Arnold was a sane and reasonable man, he gave Clara a few blemishes here and there, including slightly uneven ears and a small mole on the back of her neck. Her breasts were also a bit smaller than the average man liked, but Arnold was okay with that. He knew he didn't deserve the perfect woman, and he knew the perfect woman might someday realize he wasn't quite suited for her. He also made sure, or at least he thought until she spoke, to give her a rather shy and subordinate demeanor. Arnold certainly didn't need a wife who got any ideas.

"It's a bit late to go out," he told her with a forced yawn. "Perhaps we should just go to bed." He eyed her body up and down wondering if it was too soon to break her in.

"Okay," she said with a bit of disappointment.

Arnold walked over and gently touched her hair, but he instantly regretted this decision as a sudden longing for Claire swelled inside him.

"She's just as good, probably better," Arnold whispered to himself. Arnold saw Clara tilt her head and furrow her brow at his words.

"What was that?" he heard her say.

"Oh, nothing," he told her as he wrapped his arms around her and pulled her fresh body close to his.

"I thought you were tired," she said without reciprocating the embrace.

"I am, but you can never be too tired to hold your beautiful wife." He squeezed her a little harder as he said this, but he was still careful with her newly created body. Although confident in the way he had constructed her, one never could be too careful with new life.

"Wife?" Clara squealed.

Arnold's arms went limp and slid off her body. He took a step back and looked into her blue eyes. They looked nothing like Claire's hazel.

"Yes, wife," he assured her as if her were talking to a dog or child or robot. "You are my wife," he said again, nodding his head slowly to make sure she understood.

"Okay, if you say so," she muttered with a drop of her head.

"I do," he said.

She looked back up at him. "What's a wife?" she asked.

He wondered if she was being playful, but there was nothing in her tone that suggested so. In fact, there was nothing in her tone at all. It was almost like he'd made her atonal. That was something they would have to work on, but right now he just felt lonely and wanted to take her to bed with him.

"A wife is a woman who does everything her husband says," he told her with a firm nod of confidence. "And I am your husband," he added in anticipation of her next question.

"That sounds easy enough," she said as she offered her first smile. The dimples in her cheeks were much deeper than Claire's.

"Kiss me," he told her.

Clara moved toward him and puckered her lips. She planted a short wet kiss on his jawbone.

"On the lips," he told her trying not to sound bossy.

"Oh, sorry," she said. She puckered again and planted a kiss on his lips. Again it was short and wet, but he found it quite tantalizing nonetheless.

For a moment, Arnold was conflicted. What he had in front of him was the most amazing woman he'd ever seen. She had a killer body (except of course for those few minor flaws), and she would surely give into his every command (although it seemed like her submittal to requests would be very literal). The problem was that he just wasn't sure what he should have her do. Was it better to have her attend to his every need, making him the sandwich he desperately craved after all his hard work, or should he have her satisfy the sexual needs that had gone unquenched for the last few weeks with Claire?

It didn't take too long for Arnold to realize what he should do—he would create *another* wife. Then Clara could handle the sexual stuff while the new wife handled everything else.

"Let's take a shower," he told her with a broad smile.

"Okay," she said as she stripped off her clothes right then and there. Arnold's eyes widened at the sight of her nude body. He'd only seen a body like that in internet videos. He started to second guess his decision to create another wife, unsure he could control his libido through the hours of labor that cloning took. Of course he knew it would be worth it in the end, especially if he made a woman of Clara's equal.

Clara marched to the shower while he stood in thought, her perfect swaying body quickly turning his mind away from its troubles.

"Are you coming, husband?" she asked from the bathroom door.

"You bet I am," he told her as he hurried to the bathroom, tripping over the pants he was removing on the way. Clara let out a little laugh at his clumsiness. Arnold was embarrassed and a bit angry, but Clara's face only gave off innocence, so he decided to forgive her.

The naked pair stepped into the shower and was soon engulfed in the hot mist descending from the showerhead. Clara reached for a bottle of shampoo, but Arnold told her he'd take care of it. "Let me wash you," he said. She handed him the bottle and turned her back to the water. As he lathered the shampoo in her hair, he tugged at the strands, removing more than a few handfuls. He clumped the strands of hair together and tossed them to the shower floor. "Go ahead and rinse," he told her. The water from her hair pounded onto the tub like a mighty waterfall descending. Arnold protected the clump of hair by placing his toes on it, and the pair soaped and rinsed each other until their bodies were thoroughly cleansed.

"Ready to get out?" he asked her after the last bit of soap washed off his body.

"Whatever you say, husband," she told him.

Arnold retrieved two towels and they dried themselves. After they got out, Clara pointed to the hairball hovering near the drain.

"Ewwww," she said. "Aren't you going to take care of that?"

He almost lost his patience and told her that he gave the orders, but instead he told her that he'd take care of it in a little bit.

"Why don't you head to bed?" he told her. "I'll join you in a minute."

"Okee dokee," she said as she dropped her towel to the floor and swayed her hips off to bed. He watched her climb under the sheets without putting any clothes on. He'd always wanted to get Claire to sleep naked with him, and now he had a wife that was far sexier than Claire naked in his bed. Unfortunately he still had some work to do, but he vowed to do it quickly so he could be with Clara.

Arnold pulled the clump of hair out of the tub and set to work, creating a woman almost as perfect as Clara in appearance, but he focused a little more on her domestic skills rather than her sexual appeal.

When Arnold was just about finished, he heard Clara get out of bed.

"Don't come in," he shouted.

"Okay, but I'm lonely," Clara said before turning back and crawling under the sheets again.

"I'll be there in just a second." Arnold's loins and stomach were in near agony by this point, but everything was going to turn around for him soon. He was about to become the most satisfied man on the planet.

"There," he said as he stepped back and looked at his new creation. "I'll call you Cara," he said to the new woman. She was quite stunning as well, although she looked much less like Claire than Clara did. As he continued to ogle her, it didn't take Arnold long to realize that perhaps Cara was the more desirable woman. He decided he would just have to put them to the test. He'd have them each make him a sandwich and each sleep with him. The women would therefore decide their own fates.

"You are my wife, and your job is to do whatever I say," Arnold told Cara in a soothing voice.

"That sounds nice," Cara said. Her voice was even more robotic than Clara's, but she more than made up for it in other areas. Although he had set out to make a less perfect woman, he found Cara's features more than satisfactory for his tastes.

"You can start by meeting me in the bedroom," he told her. It was a quick change of mind, for he had thought she would make the sandwich first, but he found he couldn't control his sexual urges any longer.

"That sounds nice," Cara repeated.

Arnold bolted for the bedroom before Cara could undress. When he entered the room and saw Clara curled up under the sheets he tried to order her to make him a sandwich, but the words wouldn't come out. Instead he climbed into bed with her and wrapped one arm around her.

"Who's that?" Cara and Clara said simultaneously when Cara entered the room.

"That's my other wife," Arnold said to the two women. "Come join us," he said to Cara.

"That sounds nice," Cara said as she slipped into the bed under Arnold's other arm.

Just as Arnold was trying to decide which one to make a move on first, he heard the garage door open. At first he thought it was just his imagination, so he looked back and forth between the two beautiful clones of his wife, wondering what exactly he was going to do. He finally set his mind on Cara and whispered into her ear, "How about you—"

"What the hell is going on here?" a shrill voice inflected from the entryway to the bedroom.

Arnold's eyes widened as he saw the silhouette of Claire standing in the doorway, her suitcases sliding out of her hands and crashing onto the floor. One of them spilled open and out poured a week's worth of clothes.

"Wh-what are you doing here?" Arnold stammered as Clara and Cara both said, "Is that your wife, too?"

"My flight was cancelled, you asshole," she screamed. "I called you six times to tell you, but you never answered your damn phone so I had to take a cab." She took out her own phone and threw it at him. "And who are these two bimbos?" she demanded as she stormed over to the bed.

"We're his wife," the women said in unison.

"So is this the kind of thing you do while I'm gone on vacation?" Claire roared. "And I thought all you did was play fantasy football and jerk off." She let out a loud snort.

"Vacation?" Arnold squeaked. "I thought you were leaving me so I cloned some new wives for myself."

"Like I'm supposed to believe that," Claire screamed at her husband. "But I can tell you that I sure as hell am leaving you now. You can stuff your bed full of all the sex dolls you want. But you aren't ever going to get with me again, that's for sure."

Claire stormed out of the room without bothering to pick up her suitcases. Arnold heard the garage door close and her car peel out onto the street.

"Well, what should we do now?" Arnold asked his ladies, but they both just stared blankly at him.

Steven Storky and the Case of the Lost Balls

Steven Storky has lost his balls. His wife, Sandy, may have them, but Steven doesn't have the balls to ask her.

It'll be a lose-lose situation if he asks her anyway. She certainly won't give them back, and if she hasn't taken them, she'll be mad at him for making such an accusation. Steven thinks it's best to look for them elsewhere and only resort to asking Sandy after exhausting all other possibilities.

He's not sure exactly when he lost them. It must've been a gradual thing, like when something builds up and builds up and you aren't sure what's going on and then suddenly there's this "aha" moment like suicidal people must feel.

Steven Storky wakes up one morning after having had that building up feeling (actually, his is more of a wearing away feeling) for weeks. Three minutes before his alarm rings at 5:03 he springs up in bed and shouts, "Aha!"

Sandy slaps him in the back and shushes him. She doesn't like being disturbed, but Steven has to do it every morning at 5:03 anyway. "Just don't wake up," he tried to convince her once, but she wouldn't have any of it. She seemed much more interested in waking up and criticizing him. Steven still doesn't understand but accepts that this is the way things are. He apologizes and hurries out of bed, his work clothes neatly set out in the other room, his toothbrush and other toiletries tucked away in the cabinet beneath the sink in the guest bathroom.

When Steven takes a shower this morning, he feels down below to see if maybe those balls aren't hiding up there somewhere. His fingers can't find a trace. It's like they've simply vanished.

At work this very same day one of his co-workers says Steven doesn't seem to be all there. Steven pretends not to know what the guy is talking about. "Nope, I'm all here, every bit of me, right in this office, all here," he insists way too much. The co-worker shrugs and says something else Steven can't hear. Then Steven goes off to his cubicle to do some menial tasks his boss has requested via email. Although Steven isn't keen on the work, he's glad his boss has the courtesy to deliver the commands in a silent fashion. He would've hated having a boss who came into his cubicle and announced the tasks in front of all his co-workers. It would be embarrassing for them to hear the things he is forced to do at his age and experience level. Not that they respect him anyway, which is why he has to do the tasks to begin with.

Sitting at his desk in the cubicle pounding away at his keyboard on something trivial, it suddenly occurs to Steven that his boss might have his balls, or perhaps even one of the other employees in the office. He decides to look around for them, but the boss catches him off task and asks him what's going on. Steven mumbles something about getting coffee or making copies and the boss tells him to get back to work. After the encounter he returns to his desk and stays in the cubicle the rest of the day, skipping lunch and holding his bladder for almost three hours before stopping in the john at exactly 5:07 on his way out of the building. Once his bladder is relieved he retrieves his lunch from the office lunch room and eats his peanut butter and jelly sandwich and a granny smith apple on his walk down the five flights of stairs. He takes his final bite of apple, ripping the flesh all the way to the core so the seeds are visible, and pitches the leftovers in a garbage can in the parking lot. Then he strolls to his light blue sedan. The blue is so light that most people think the car is white or dirty or maybe even an odd shade of green. Actually, the blue is so light that most people don't even notice the car at all.

On the drive home from work, Steven sees a Welsh Corgi walking with what appears to be a ball in its mouth. Steven thinks it's one of his so he slams on his brakes and veers to the curb. As he gets out of the car a small boy with a red baseball cap takes the ball out of the dog's mouth and walks away. "Hey, that's my ball!" Steven shouts at the boy. The boy continues to walk away. The Corgi doesn't seem to belong to the boy. Steven doesn't bother to turn off the engine and starts chasing the boy on foot. "Give me my ball!" Steven yells. The boy runs faster, fast enough to make his red cap fall off. Steven runs past it and chases the boy for two and a half blocks before the boy cuts up a yard and starts knocking on a door. While the boy waits on the porch Steven slows to a walk and then stands still by a fire hydrant. The door opens and the boy goes inside. Steven contemplates marching to the door and demanding his ball. He walks halfway to the door but sees the curtains flicker in the window so he turns around and heads back to his car, picking up the red hat on the way and placing it upon his head.

A police officer is waiting by the idling car with a pad of tickets. She removes one and puts it underneath his wiper blade. He wants to argue but knows he was probably in the wrong even though it wasn't his fault. He doesn't know how to explain why he left the car there. The Corgi is gone. With a tip of his new tight red hat he apologizes to the officer and gets in the car, grabbing the ticket from the windshield before sitting.

Steven goes out of his way to drive by the house the kid entered. When he doesn't see any activity, he turns his car around and drives by again. The house is still silent. He makes a mental note of the address and decides he will send them a letter. As he drives home he keeps his eye out for any sign of his other ball, but all he sees is a shirtless jogger with a very hairy chest and a man collecting cans in a shopping cart. In his mind he tells the jogger to put on a shirt and the can-man to find a real job. Out loud he mumbles the wrong words to a Rolling Stones song playing on the radio.

When he opens his garage door and pulls into the driveway something on the roof catches his eye. It's definitely his other ball. He wonders how the two got so far apart. He leaves the car idling in the driveway and yanks the ladder out of the garage. Once it's sturdily resting against the side of the house, he climbs the rungs without thinking about ladder safety. The car's engine whirrs beneath him. Sandy comes out the front door and asks what the hell he's doing just as he places his left foot on the roof.

"I saw something on the roof," he calls down to her.

"Hurry the hell up," she tells him. "Dinner's almost ready, you're wasting gas, and you look like a buffoon on the roof in your work clothes."

Steven doesn't dispute any of these facts. He looks down at his black wingtips, khaki slacks, blue shirt, and navy sport coat and knows he doesn't belong on the roof. "I'll only be a minute," is all he says in reply.

His hesitation in listening to Sandy and bothering to reply proves rather costly. A large black bird lets out a brief "caw." The ball, which is no more than seven feet away from his wingtip, is suddenly scooped up in the black bird's beak. It's a snug fit, but the bird manages, holding onto the sphere with ease as it flies into a nest in the neighbor's elm tree. "Hey, that's my ball!" Steven yells at the bird.

"What are you talking about?" Sandy calls from the ground below. Steven hadn't known she was still there. He pretends he doesn't hear her and comes down the ladder.

"Did you get the thing off the roof?" she asks when he's on the ground.

"A bird took it," he says sliding the ladder back into the garage.

"What was it?"

Steven wonders if she already knows what it is. He thinks she might've put it up there to begin with, but he's not sure why she would do such a thing.

"It looked like a ball," he says.

"What kind of ball?" she persists. He wonders why she cares so much.

"A round one," he says in an attempt to be funny.

Sandy doesn't laugh. "Where is it now?"

"A bird took it," he tells her. He wonders if she will care that a bird has her husband's ball, figuring she would probably want to keep it for herself.

"Must not've been a very big ball," she mutters as she turns to go back inside.

Steven makes mocking gestures with his mouth while pulling the car into the garage. He tries to think of a way to get back at Sandy, but mostly he wants to get his balls back. Even just one would be nice.

After parking the car in the garage he goes over to his neighbor's house and rings the doorbell.

The neighbor comes outside and politely asks what he wants. Steven is sure the neighbor is only pretending to be friendly.

"A bird in your tree has something of mine," Steven tells him.

The neighbor stops pretending. "What do you want me to do about it?"

"I was wondering if you wouldn't mind if I climbed up your tree to get it out," Steven says.

"What is it?" The neighbor puts his hand on the door.

"It's a ball," Steven says. He begins to think his neighbor is in on the whole thing. Sandy probably had this guy take the balls. Lord knows she doesn't like to touch down there these days.

"What kind of ball?" the neighbor asks.

Steven looks around for a moment and then leans in. "It's *my* ball," he whispers to the neighbor.

"Well no shit," the neighbor says.

Steven thinks his suspicions are confirmed.

"I want it back," Steven says.

"Well, knock yourself out," the neighbor says. "But if you damage my tree you're paying for it."

Just as the neighbor closes the door Steven sees the bird fly away. He thinks he sees the ball in its beak. He reaches out to ring the doorbell again to let the neighbor know he isn't going to bother with the tree, but he decides against it. There's a chance he'll go up the tree later after the bird returns.

Steven goes inside his own house and smells dinner. Sandy has cooked a roast and is serving mashed potatoes and carrots with it. Steven says it smells good. He knows she'll claim to have slaved over it if he doesn't, but he knows it's really just something she threw in the oven at four o'clock when she got home from work. The potatoes are just the instant kind, but he actually thinks they taste better than the real ones she mashes up on special occasions.

"Why did you go to the Perry's" house?" Sandy asks.

Steven hesitates. He thinks it might be a trap, but he can't think of a good lie so he just tells her that he wanted to ask about the ball.

"Why do you care so much about this stupid ball?" Sandy asks. The way she says it makes Steven think that maybe she didn't put it up there and that maybe she doesn't know exactly which ball he's talking about.

"I just need it, that's all," Steven says.

"For what?" she asks.

Steven can't think of anything he really needs it for, but he knows it would be nice to have. He shrugs and says, "Never mind, let's just eat." The couple sits in silence save for the occasional comment about their respective days.

After an evening of watching television on separate couch cushions, Sandy tells Steven it's time for bed. Steven isn't tired, so he tells her he is going to stay up for a bit.

"What for?" she asks.

Steven is getting tired of her questions.

"To get some stuff done," he tells her.

"What stuff do you have to do?" She stares at him with her hands on her hips.

"Don't worry about it," he tells her. She continues to stare. He thinks about apologizing but decides just to go do some stuff on the computer. He doesn't notice her facial expression. All he knows is she doesn't ask him anything else.

Steven putzes around on the computer for a while not really accomplishing much of anything but having a good time nonetheless. Before going to bed he takes a leak. Just for old time's sake he feels around down there. His fingers detect a pea-sized development on each side. He wonders if they were there this morning and he just hadn't noticed.

At 5:02 the next morning he springs out of bed, making plenty of noise in the process. Sandy swings at his back but misses. He doesn't apologize for waking her. He goes into the bathroom and feels around again. Now he feels a couple marbles down there. It's unmistakable that the lumps have gotten bigger. He smiles as he reaches into the cabinet beneath the guest sink for his deodorant. A mason jar behind the pipes catches his eye. He pulls it out and examines the contents. There are two balls floating around in a murky liquid. He feels down below again. The marbles are still there. He thinks about the Corgi and the boy with the red cap and the police officer and the bird and his neighbor. He wonders whose balls are in the jar. They don't look familiar, not like the ones he saw yesterday.

He takes the lid off and smells the contents. His body recoils at the stench. These have been in the jar for more than a few days. He almost marches into the bedroom to demand whose balls are in the jar, but then he has second thoughts. Instead he opens the toilet lid and dumps everything, liquid, balls and all, into the bowl. He flushes, watching the toilet gurgle as it sucks down the balls. Just for good measure, he feels himself again. The marbles are still there. He sets down the mason jar proudly and pulls on his underwear all the while wondering when his balls will be back to full size. Then he hears his wife stirring in the other room. He pulls off his underwear and struts to the bedroom door, knowing just how he can get his balls back.

The Ugly Husband

One Tuesday morning Jessica Bruno awoke to find a very ugly man lying beside her.

Panic overtook her and she curled into a fetal position. Three times she closed her eyes. Three times she reopened them. Three times the same unfortunate-looking male breathed inches from her face.

At first she thought it was a terrible mistake.

I must've gotten drunk last night, she told herself.

She was about to roll over, wondering how to explain her overnight absence to her husband, when she noticed the unmistakable painting. An exploding sailboat pierced by a horned whale.

Okay, so I've slept with another man in our marriage bed.

Fearing the doom she would face when she opened the bedroom door and encountered her rightfully enraged husband, she decided to take another look at the man. Perhaps he wasn't that ugly.

Her first glance had not deceived her. The man was indeed hideous. His face was like nothing she had seen before. God must have created this man out of spite. Here she was trapped in the sheets with him. Fortunately the man was still sleeping, but his breath was a vile concoction of burnt rubber, raw sewage and rotten eggs. She slowly brought her hand to her nostrils, trying not to disturb the slumbering beast.

She began to roll away, unable to take the stench emitted from his jaw. At her movement, the beast began to stir. She had disturbed the hideous creature.

"Good morning sweetheart," cawed the beast with a smile no woman could possibly adore.

She shut her eyes, hoping the monster had not spotted her.

He planted a kiss on her head. "Wake up sleepyhead. Today we leave for Mexico."

She flung open her eyes as the truth sank into her already terrified mind. This was no simple mistake. The repulsive thing in the bed beside her was her husband, the man she had happily married seven years ago.

How did I not realize this before?

Douglas slid his arm around her body.

Jessica recoiled. "I have to go to the bathroom," she said, flinging the sheets onto his face in a desperate attempt at magic.

In the security of the tiled room she looked about for an explanation. Was her husband really that ugly? The picture from their honeymoon fastened to the mirror confirmed he was. The rose-colored goggles had come off. Love was no longer blind. The man was truly ugly in every fathomable way and she had made the incurable error of agreeing to spend the rest of her life with him.

There were few options:

Divorce was messy and unappealing.

She could constantly live a lie, pretend she hadn't married a grotesque creature, close her eyes and imagine someone else, anyone else, every time she kissed him or made love to him. Such willful ignorance would surely have its limitations.

In reality there was no hope; she would simply have to live with the fact that someone had once lied to her and told her that what was on the inside counted a lot more than the way somebody looked.

Then it came to her. She could blind herself.

Yes, that was what she would do. The physical pain would pale in comparison to the agonizing torture she would experience every day for the rest of her life. She just had to choose the right tool to make it look like an accident.

The options overwhelmed her.

I'll stab myself with nail clippers was her first thought, but that seemed painful, messy and unexplainable.

I'll burn my eyes with the curling iron was the next thought that came, but she was afraid of the scars.

I'll smash my head into the mirror. Again, messy, and she didn't want brain damage to accompany her blindness.

I'll spray my eyes with Lysol until I can't see anymore.

She thought for a while, but there were no flaws. Lysol would burn away the problems of her husband's ugliness.

A few sprays later she was writhing in pain on the floor. Douglas rushed in when he heard her screams.

"I'm blind! I'm blind!" she shouted.

After flushing her eyes with water, he rushed her to the hospital, holding her hand tenderly all the while.

She grasped his hand tightly to relieve some of the pain.

She was not surprised when the doctor walked into the room and said, "I'm afraid you're blind, Mrs. Bruno. The damage is permanent. There were just too many toxins."

A curious crooked smile crept across her face.

When the doctor left, she listened as Douglas spoke, trying to comfort her, trying to get the details of the accident. "I just don't understand how something like this could have happened," he said.

"Because you are so ugly," she muttered to herself, forgetting for a moment that the man she couldn't see was standing next to her and perfectly capable of hearing.

As they stood in silence, she could feel his ugly staring face much more vividly than she ever had before. It was so ugly.

The Flaming Skull

Mark Nipple stood in the living room, the lottery ticket tucked away in his pocket. His green Sex Pistols tee clung raggedly to his plumped torso. An inked skull's stretched jaw smiled strangely beneath the shirt's cuff. He really hoped today would be his lucky day.

He didn't need to look at the ticket to check the numbers. They were always the same. The combination of numbers from various facts revolving around the lives of Johnny Rotten and Sid Vicious were more permanent than the skull on his arm.

The numbers came up. "Fuck!" Mark yelled at the television. Not a single one. He never got a single one. It was like those numbers were cursed.

"Can you fix the bookshelf today?" his wife Anita called from the kitchen.

"Fuck," he muttered, hoping she wouldn't hear him.

"What was that?"

"Nothing," he mumbled.

"Good. Then fix the bookshelf. Aubrey's coming over for dinner tonight and I don't want the house looking a mess."

Mark looked at the bookshelf. It was a little crooked, but it wasn't that bad. It's not like shit was falling off, he thought to himself. Besides, Aubrey doesn't care about that. It's not like he's a carpenter.

"I'll fix it if I have time," he found himself saying.

"And why wouldn't you have time?" Anita closed a cabinet hard. Mark pretended it'd just slipped.

"I'm working on some songs today," he said.

"You've got to be kidding," Anita said.

Mark stumbled for justification. "Yeah, I was going to help Aubrey. He's got some audition coming up, and I want him to have it down pat. He could make it big, you know. The kid's mighty good. He's almost as good as I was."

"Are you still hung up on that band thing?" Anita asked. "Not everyone's meant to be a rock star. It just wasn't for you." She walked out of the kitchen.

"Besides, you've made a mark on the music industry. Look at all those great covers you designed." She pointed to one on the bookshelf.

Mark glanced at the album art and scoffed. "We didn't make it because we didn't want to make it," Mark said. "We coulda been huge if we wanted it. Camelback Toepatch wasn't about being huge."

"Of course you could have, honey," Anita said. "But you've got to follow your heart."

Mark laughed to himself. Like she knew what was in his heart. She didn't even know about the damn lottery tickets.

"Why are you wearing that stupid shirt? Make sure you change if you leave the house," she said. "You live in Pittsburgh. Why do you care about anarchy in the U.K.?"

Mark reached into his pocket and crumbled the lottery ticket. He took a good hard look at his wife and imagined the first time he saw her. He was up on stage sweating and doing that thing with his tongue that drove her crazy. Anita had almost fallen to her knees. After the show he jumped off the stage and pulled her out of the little club and into his station wagon. He'd never had such a wild lay in his life. Now he looked at her and saw someone who wanted to fix bookshelves on the weekend. He just wanted to win the lottery, get the band back together, tour the world, and screw his wife sideways in seven different positions on a personalized bus. He didn't want to fix any bookshelves or design graphic art for other people's album covers.

"I'm going to get my hair done before Aubrey gets here," she said. "Make sure it's fixed before I get back."

She blew him an unseductive kiss, grabbed her purse, and headed out to the car. Mark didn't bother to return the kiss. He thought about pulling out some old pictures of her, the ones she used to give him before they were married, but he didn't feel like putting out the effort. Instead he went down to the basement and grabbed his old Fender. He strummed a C chord and found it was horribly out of tune, like it hadn't been played since the Sex Pistols broke up. Mark fumbled with the pegs for a moment before giving up. He didn't have the ear for that anymore anyway. Besides, no one was listening.

He brought the guitar and his old Honeywell amp up to the living room. After plugging the amp in next to the bookshelf, he flipped it on and gave the guitar a good whack. Some trinkets on the bookshelf vibrated. Mark glanced at them and the album cover caught his eye. The color scheme was mighty impressive, he had to admit, but the album itself was shit. He didn't understand how something like that could be released on a major label when his band couldn't even get signed by an independent. It was all bullshit, all politics, all shit that Johnny Rotten hated, so Mark should've hated it too. But he didn't.

His left hand choked the neck of the guitar and he pounded the strings a dozen times. The bookshelf rattled and one of the crooked shelves slid down a little more. Mark wanted it to fall, for all the glass shit to spill off and shatter.

While the cacophony of chords still rumbled, Mark stalked closer to the amp to create the signature feedback that Camelback Toepatch invented long before those grungy punk-wannabes from Seattle got famous.

The screech of the feedback tortured Mark's aging ears, but he smiled nonetheless and dropped to his knees. Mark miscalculated the effect gravity would have on him, and his body lunged into the amplifier, sandwiching the guitar between himself and the blood-shrieking speaker. A moment of dull ache reverberated through his stomach before he felt the fading skull on his bicep erupt into flames.

Still on the amp, Mark looked at the burning tattoo on his arm. It had never looked so alive. He knew it should've hurt like hell, but it energized him instead. He rose, and without bothering to tune the guitar, he launched into a feedback-ridden guitar solo that would've left any punk fans both cringing and thrashing until their bodies dropped exhausted to the sweat-covered floor.

Mark spent the next hour slamming power chords and shredding the strings until his fingertips had been stripped clean of flesh. The skull on his arm continued to flame. For his epic encore, Mark axe-chopped the guitar into the bookshelf and watched the wood splinter as the shelf's contents, album cover included, spilled to the floor in a drowning panic.

In that moment, Mark knew Camelback Toepatch was indeed destined for greatness. The forever burning skull on his arm promised him such fame. Unfortunately for Mark, the creaking of the rusty garage door springs did not promise or even support any such idea. In walked Anita, her new hairstyle rigid and unwelcoming. The hair said, and in a stern way, not to fuck around. Mark felt it scolding him, and he wanted to light it on fire with his tattoo. But when he held up his arm to ignite the hair, he noticed the flame had gone out. The skull was fading. He turned away from his nonplussed wife and picked up the guitar. A hard strum produced only a feeble sound.

"I thought I told you to fix the fucking bookshelf," his wife, or maybe her hair, yelled from the doorway.

She stomped over to him and ripped the guitar out of his sweaty and trembling hands. She swung it at the amp. The neck split from the body. She threw the neck at him. "Now fix the fucking bookshelf!"

Mark looked at his arm and noticed the tattoo was almost invisible now.

"And take off that fucking shirt! We're in Pittsburgh in 2012 for Christ sake."

Mark changed his shirt and fixed the bookshelf, grumbling the whole time. Then he tossed out the broken amp and split guitar.

At dinner that night Aubrey asked if he'd been playing the guitar at all lately. Mark didn't bother answering. Then Aubrey dropped the big news.

"I got signed!" he squealed.

Mark wanted to be happy, but all he felt was emptiness. He started to hum a Camelback Toepatch song, but his wife shushed him and told Aubrey to tell his story. Then Mark noticed his tattoo was completely gone.

Edwin and the Mannequins

Edwin McGee loved to ogle the mannequins outside of Victoria's Secret. He wasn't sure what he found so appealing about them. Yes, they had mountains for breasts, and those mountains were always covered with something lacey or silky or feathery or ruffly, but other than that, there wasn't much to them.

Still, every time he went to the mall, whether alone, with a group of friends, or even with his wife, Edwin McGee made sure he walked past the storefront at least four times, and he never tried to hide his lustful stares.

"Why must you do that?" his wife, Erin, asked him once when his stare bordered on complete fixation. It was so bad that he had actually come to a stand still and was undressing the mannequin with his eyes. He was no better than a kid by a toy store window near Christmas time. In fact, he was far worse. At least there was something innocent about the kid and the toy store.

"I was just picturing you wearing that," he finally said after she nudged him twice.

"If you want to see me in it, then why don't you buy it for me?" Erin asked with a hint of longing in her voice.

That gave Edwin an idea.

The next day Edwin returned to the mall and went straight inside Victoria's Secret. Although he had passed the store thousands of times, it was the first time he'd ever been inside. He was impressed by the vast array of pinks and whites and reds that swirled all around the store. He wasn't impressed by the countless obese and unattractive women who were fondling the skimpy unmentionables.

After almost telling one particularly large woman not to bother with her purchase, Edwin became entranced by one of the mannequins. He had studied them all extensively before, at least the ones in the storefront window, but he had never seen this specimen. It was dressed in a piece of silken orange fabric that hung delicately from the breasts to the waistline. There were silver sequins all around the nipple area, and below the bosom the sheered piece flared out ever so slightly. He wanted to go blow on it and watch it ripple in his wind.

"Can I help you?" a woman asked while he stared at the headless mannequin.

The woman's voice broke him from the trance. He wanted to pretend it was the mannequin's voice, but it was far too deep to belong to such a beautiful creature.

Edwin didn't bother to look at the employee that had spoken to him, but he assumed that she looked nothing like any of the models pictured outside. "I'll take that one," he said with a point just as the woman was about to walk away.

"Excellent choice," she said insincerely. "What size would you like?"

"I want *that* one," he said again.

"Sir, we have plenty more in stock in all sizes. We'd prefer not to sell the display unless we're all out." The woman had a patient tone to her voice, and Edwin appreciated that. But it also occurred to him that they were talking about two different things.

"I don't want to buy just the lingerie," he said, finally turning to look at her. "I want the whole thing."

She scrunched her eyes and turned her head slightly. "Do you mean that you want the mannequin?"

"Yes," he replied. "I'd like to buy your mannequin."

The woman shook her head. He noticed from her name tag that she went by Amber.

"I'm not sure we can do that," Amber told him.

"Can you check for me, Amber?"

Amber walked away for a moment, presumably to find a manager. While she was gone Edwin stepped a little closer to the mannequin. He wanted to smell it, but he figured he would just wait until he got it home. He closed his eyes and began to imagine its scent and what he might do with it. Hopefully his wife would let him bring it into the bed.

While he was lost in his fantasy, Amber returned with a tall blonde woman.

"How may I help you sir?" the new woman asked Edwin.

Edwin opened his eyes and looked at the new woman. She looked a little more like someone who might work at a lingerie store that touted itself as being the sexiest place to buy skimpy clothing.

"I would like to buy that one," he said with a point. His finger quivered before the mannequin.

"I'm sorry, sir, but our mannequins are not for sale. They are for display only." The woman seemed very impatient. Edwin could tell that she did not value his business.

"I can make it worth your while," he said in a voice that came out more seductive than he intended.

"Sir, I am going to have to ask you to leave the store," the woman replied. She reached for her cell phone to show she meant business.

Not one for making a scene, Edwin left of his own accord, strolling slowly by the window once he had exited. He tried to get a final glance at his dream girl, but the piece wasn't visible through the window. He settled for the lesser specimens available for all passersby to see. It struck him as odd that they wouldn't put their finest mannequin in the window, but he also realized that it made her all the more special.

Edwin couldn't sleep that night. His mind would not leave the Victoria's Secret store. The image of that beautiful mannequin remained stuck in his head no matter what else he tried to think about. At one point he even propositioned his wife for sex, but she turned him down with a gentle swat. Her refusal didn't really bother him; he wasn't in the mood anyway. It just pained him to think of the woman he couldn't have.

Then another idea came to him.

"Where are you going?" his wife mumbled as he climbed out of bed and put on his pants.

"Don't worry about it," he told her.

She didn't seem to.

Less than an hour later Edwin found himself outside the mall. He drove his car behind the building by the shipping and loading doors. After finding the one for Victoria's Secret, he parked his car and walked up to the door with a crowbar in his hand. He worked at the door for a few minutes before it popped open. An alarm sounded, so he knew he didn't have much time.

In a panic, and without the aid of lights, Edwin ran to the spot where he thought he had seen his mannequin. With little effort he grabbed it and bolted out of the store through the backdoor. He managed to get into his car and drive away before any mall security approached him. A successful heist, or so he thought.

Halfway home, he looked over at the passenger in his car and saw a turquoise bra.

"What the hell?" he yelled as he slammed on the breaks in the middle of the road. He glared at the mannequin. She was the least attractive he had ever seen from the Victoria's Secret collection. "Where the hell is my girl?" he shouted at the mannequin.

It didn't answer.

"Get the hell out of my car?" he roared at the motionless plaster

The mannequin didn't move.

Edwin opened the door and shoved her out of the car. He pulled the door shut and sped off, the mannequin and her turquoise lingerie left stranded in the middle of the road. Just as he pulled away from it, rain began to pour down from the sky.

"Bitch!" he screamed. Edwin felt cheated. He wondered if the employees had rearranged the store just so he wouldn't have easy access to his love. He had been so certain of where his mannequin had been in the store. Those evil women must've done this to him. Somehow they knew he would come back.

"Where did you go?" his wife asked when he returned to bed.

"I told you not to worry about it," he said, still shaking and sweating from the failed abduction.

"Whatever," she said before rolling on to her side and falling back to sleep. He tried to follow suit, but he couldn't stop picturing all of the Victoria's Secret mannequins in a room staring at him. They all pointed and laughed because he couldn't find his dream girl. To make matters worse, they were all wearing sheer orange lingerie. It was horrifying.

"You look like shit," Edwin's wife said in the morning.

Edwin didn't take this as offensive. He felt like shit, and smelled like it too.

"Are you okay?" she asked him.

He stared at her for a few minutes, debating whether he should tell her about the previous night's affairs. Her loving glance told him it was best not to say anything. "Just didn't sleep well, that's all," was all he said.

"Well, I've got a surprise for you," she told him.

"Okay," he managed, still a little shaken.

"I'll just go get it," she said before leaving the room.

Edwin tried to doze off while she was away, but sleep didn't come. He kept his eyes closed until he heard her voice.

"What do you think?" she cooed, his eyes springing open at the sudden sexiness of her voice.

When he opened his eyes, there his wife stood, wearing nothing but a thin piece of orange fabric with silver sequins around the nipples.

"*You* did it!" Edwin shouted at her when he recognized the threads she wore. "*You* killed my love!" he screamed again.

Edwin jumped out of bed and began ransacking the house looking for his mannequin.

"What are you doing?" his wife asked, tears streaming down her face and soaking the sheer fabric causing it to cling tightly to her skin.

"Where did you put her?"

"I don't know what you're talking about," she said as she followed the madman around the house.

He continued to tear apart everything until, at long last, he found a small piece of white plaster on the floor of the garage. The color matched that of his beloved mannequin perfectly. Edwin fell to the ground and cried at the loss of his beautiful mannequin. His wife removed the lingerie and tossed it at him before storming off to their bedroom in the nude.

She told him she was filing for divorce when the police showed up a few hours later to question her for murder. He said that would be fine as long as he got to keep the sexy orange lingerie. He could always build another mannequin, he decided.

A Grand Unfurling

As Henry Forrester finished drying off his cherry red Ford, something caught his eye. His once vigorous arm movements slowed until the yellow cloth in his hand ceased its movement entirely, resting obliviously beside a stubborn water spot. Henry's gaze was held not by the beauty of his car but by the simplicity of cloth hanging from a wooden pole on the porch. Barely moving in the ever-so-slight breeze, the red white and blue of the flag appeared worn out, the colors almost indistinguishable. The flag was so tattered and furled that it could hardly catch a breeze if it tried. Henry might as well have just hung the drying cloth in its place.

Rag still in hand, Henry scanned the neighborhood surrounding his family's three bedroom house on Huntford Lane. The Forresters, like everyone else on their block, had kept their flag flying in all its glory since that fateful day nearly eight years ago when patriotism had suddenly become en vogue again. Across the street, the Douglasses' flag flew freely, gliding magnificently on even a gentle breeze. Next door, the Trowelers had a flag dangled with unfrayed edges and vivid colors. The David residence featured a faded flag, but it looked vintage rather than deceased. The flag at the Brayford home, the biggest on the block, didn't fly freely and had a few tatters, but the colors were filled with passion and the tears added character, as if telling the world that this flag was purposeful. Henry felt surrounded by flags that were superior to his.

Leaving the yellow cloth on the hood, he trotted up the concrete walk. Henry pushed his way into the door, not bothering to wipe his Converse shoes on the mat that welcomed him, and stormed into the foyer and subsequent hallway. "Honey," he shouted at the wife who was dusting the furniture in the living room.

"Yes, dear?"

"I need your keys." Henry was panting.

"What do you need *now*?"

Henry had already borrowed her car twice that morning, once to buy wax and once to buy a new yellow terry cloth to dry the car without leaving all the little particles that a regular rag left.

"I need to get a new flag," he said proudly.

"Why do we need a new flag? We have a flag outside already."

"Yeah, have you seen that thing? It's a total disaster. It's shameful to the country."

"Well, that's what happens when you insist on leaving it out *all* the time. Whatever happened to the notion that you were supposed to bring the flag in at sundown?" She resumed her dusting, gliding around the room and eliminating dust particles with graceful dexterity.

"Well, all the neighbors leave their flags out, and their flags all put ours to shame." Henry wanted to tear the rag out of her hand and shake all of the dust back out onto the furniture.

"So this is about pride rather than patriotism?" she asked without raising her head from the book case.

Henry paused for a second to gather his thoughts. He had never viewed himself as especially patriotic, nor had he gone out of his way to instill patriotism in his two children. But he did believe in supporting his country when he could.

"If you want a flag that badly, just take your car," she said.

"I'm not taking the Ford. I just washed it." Henry threw up his arms in disbelief.

"It's going to get dirty eventually anyway."

"So are those shelves."

"Well, I'm not refusing to use them."

"So just because I know something is going to get dirty eventually I should get it dirty right away?"

"Does that mean you are going to keep the new flag wrapped in the original packaging and save it for a special occasion?"

"You're missing the point. I worked hard to get the car to look like that. It would be like if you dusted the shelves and then poured dust all over them. Only a lot worse because it's harder to clean a car than it is to dust."

"Then next weekend we can trade," she said before playfully snapping the dust rag at him.

"Just give me your keys."

"Fine, if that's how it has to be." There was a glimmer of victory in her hazel eyes. "They're in my purse. The red one."

"Alright. Do you think I should go to Home Depot or Lowe's?"

"I don't think it really matters," she said as she opened the back door to shake the rest of the dust off into the open air. "I doubt there's a flag shortage," she added, her voice barely audible from the edge of the deck.

"Home Depot it is," he said to himself as he turned to retrieve the keys from her red purse.

As Henry backed the silver SUV down the driveway, he took one last look at the flag that hung so pathetically from the front of their house. "The neighbors must think I don't care," he said as he shifted the car into drive and pulled away.

Once inside Home Depot, Henry was momentarily overwhelmed by the vastness of the warehouse. He didn't precisely know where to look to find the flags, but he knew it best to not ask anyone. Although it was part of an employee's job to help the customers, it was also part of the customer's job, especially at a place like Home Depot, to know exactly where to go.

After strolling through the expansive store, he found a section of lawn décor, which seemed to him the most appropriate spot to garner the flags. He glanced around the area, spotting heavy concrete frogs, wooden Uncle Sams, welcome mats with various greetings, and many other items, but no flags were in sight.

"Do you need some help finding something?" an old man in an orange vest said in a friendly voice.

"Yes," Henry began, his eyes still wandering about in a last effort to spot his need. After a long pause he added, "I am looking for flags."

"We have a wide variety of flags right this way." The man led him to the next aisle where shelves and boxes were stashed with colorful flags and banners. Some were patriotic, and others were decorative, but none of them were *The* American Flag.

"No, I am looking for The Flag," Henry stated proudly. "I want a brand new American flag. The highest quality you have. One with the big silver eagle on top of the pole."

The old vested man hesitated for a moment, scratching his head with one hand and clinging to his vest pocket with the other. "I'm sorry sir, but we don't have any American flags. We're sold out. But we should get a shipment in next week."

"Sold out of flags? How can that be? Is someone hoarding them? I saw dozens of homes without flags on the way here."

"Perhaps they came when we were sold out of flags as well."

"This is ridiculous," Henry roared. "I'm an American citizen in an American store. I deserve the right to an American flag now."

"If you need a flag that badly, you can always go to another store. But what's the rush? We'll have them next week. What do you need a flag for right now? Are you heading into battle or something?" the man asked before walking away.

Disgusted, Henry marched out of the store vowing that he would never go there again.

When Henry arrived home, he noticed the flag had been removed from the porch.

"Where's the flag?" Henry inquired the moment he stepped into the door.

"I got rid of it."

"What do you mean you got rid of it?"

"I mean I disposed of it. After all, you were buying a new one."

"What did you do with it?"

"What's it matter. We have a new one now."

"No. They were all sold out."

"Sold out of flags? That's so bizarre."

"Yeah. Sold out. And now we're the fools on the block without a flag."

"It's okay. We'll just buy one the next time we go to a store that has one. We can go a few days without flying the flag."

Henry thought about her suggestion. Although he wasn't quite sure, he supposed there was nothing he could do about it now. He wasn't going to run all over town looking for a flag, especially not on his day off.

"Alright, we'll pick one up later."

For the next few weeks, Henry went about his business, forgetting all about his sudden need for a new flag. Every day came and went the same as it had before. Not having a flag made no difference in Henry's world.

One morning when Henry was sitting at work, it occurred to him that the Fourth of July was nearing much more rapidly than he had realized. Instead of feeling joy about his three day weekend, he felt a nagging sickness in his stomach. Something was dreadfully wrong, but he couldn't put his finger on what it was. For the rest of the day he sat isolated in his cubicle, skipping out on his lunch break and *both* of his coffee breaks, desperately racking his brain. At first he thought that perhaps he had missed his anniversary or his wife's birthday, but then he checked his desk calendar and verified he still had months before those dates. Perhaps there was a big family trip planned. Or a piano recital for one of the kids. Somehow he would have to get the information out of his wife when he arrived home.

Henry's car ride home was so tense with trying to remember that he almost ran two red lights. "What the hell am I forgetting?" he shouted three times during a five block stretch, passing the same number of Walgreen's stores in the process.

He was only three houses from his own when he realized what was wrong. "I need a damn flag," he shouted at the steering wheel with his arms raised. The steering wheel turned slightly to the right in response, showing either indifference or pointing to a neighbor's boldly waving flag. Henry corrected the wheel and guided the vehicle into his driveway.

"How was your day, honey?" his wife asked.

"It was the worst day of my life," he replied. "I spent the whole day trying to figure something out, and then I figured it out on the way home. It was complete agony."

"Well, glad to hear you remembered. What was it?" she asked while chopping carrots.

"We never bought that flag."

"Well, let's put dinner on hold and rush out to buy it," she said with great urgency but without dropping her knife.

"That sounds great. I just need to take a leak before we leave."

"I was just kidding dear. There will still be flags after dinner."

"Oh really? You think so? Last time you told me there was no shortage of flags, that it didn't matter where I went, and then there were no flags. The Fourth is only a few days away and we still don't have a flag. Do you want to be known as the flagless fools? I'm buying a flag right now."

"Suit yourself. I'm going to stay here and eat a hot dinner with the kids."

"Alright, don't help me out any. I'll make sure the family stays afloat."

"I'm glad you're doing your part to save our family and the country," the wife told him as she rinsed off the knife.

Not sensing the sarcasm, he nodded assertively to acknowledge her compliment and darted for the door. "I'm going to Lowe's this time. Home Depot can kiss my ass."

"Yes, I'm sure the men in blue vests will be much more helpful than the ones in orange," the wife said as she emptied the carrots into a glass bowl.

Henry didn't bother to tell her that they wore red vests at Lowe's before he slammed the door.

Henry returned home forty minutes later with a boastful look on his face.

"Where's the flag?" his wife asked.

"It's in the garage. I'm going to wait until the Fourth to put it out. It's going to really shock the neighbors. It's one helluva flag."

"That's great to hear honey. I am sure that everyone in the neighborhood will have flag envy. You know what? We should host a neighborhood barbecue to christen this momentous purchase. You were so right. Rushing out to get a flag was much more worthwhile than a dinner with your family."

He gave her a firm kiss on the cheek and a gentle slap on the bottom. "That's a great idea honey. You can call the neighbors tomorrow and let them know."

"You want me to tell them about your flag?"

"No, you're gonna invite them to the party." With these words he rushed upstairs to change, loosening both his tie and his belt on the way.

When the big day finally rolled around—Henry had utilized his obligatory day off from work on the observed holiday by playing golf while his wife went to the grocery store and lugged watermelons, cases of Budweiser, and packages of meat into the house—the Forresters were prepared to throw the best Fourth of July party the neighborhood had ever seen.

While his neighbors wiped barbecue sauce off their hands onto disposable American flag napkins, Henry went to the garage to retrieve the guest of honor. He had thought about unveiling the new flag before the guests arrived, but he wanted to see the looks on their faces as he unraveled the majestic cloth in front of them.

With the tightly packaged phallus held in his firm grip, he marched like a soldier out of the garage and into the backyard where his neighbors were feasting. "Excuse me everyone," Henry bellowed proudly.

The crowd looked with mild interest at him as they continued to eat.

"I'd like to cap off this fine celebration with a brief remembrance of what this day is all about." He cleared his throat regally. "Please follow me," he added as he turned to lead the dozen feasters to the front of the house.

Henry ascended the few steps up to the porch. Like a knight, he unsheathed the flag from the transparent cellophane, his hand just above the grand eagle that sat with wings spread atop the pole, guarding the mighty stars and stripes with its menacing talons.

Henry imagined oohs and aahs as he slid his hands down the fine cedar shaft. In one grandiose swing, the flag unfurled with exceeding power, cutting through the wind, its stars and stripes in such vibrant colors that he could see the entire history of his country in each minute detail. He waved the flag twice more, its thick cloth beating powerfully against the wind like the wings of a great bird. In one swooping motion, he slid the wooden pole into the metal holder that had served the old flag so well. The flag securely in place, he stepped back and offered a salute, a few tears glistening in his eyes as he prepared for the grand finale. He bent over and pressed the play button on a hidden Sony boom box. Within seconds, "God Bless America" blared from the crackly speakers of the portable stereo. As the song filled the neighborhood, Henry raised his hands like a conductor to prompt the small crowd to join this fine celebration of the greatest country in the world.

He stood in his grand posture through the final note, holding it out himself longer than the backing tape, the flag still full sail in the breeze. When he could no longer hold the note, he erupted into an applause that was reciprocated half-heartedly by his neighbors, most of whom still munched on potato salad and watermelon.

"And now for dessert," his wife suddenly chirped. "You're all going to just love what I've made," she said in the bubbliest voice she could offer.

The neighbors turned to follow her, and Henry, content with his display, marched down the steps methodically, wondering all the while what the dessert was.

As he turned the corner to head to the backyard, a strong gust of wind roared through Huntford Lane, its force ripping the old rusty flagpole hanger right off the wooden pillar. The flag flopped to the ground like a wounded aircraft, smacking first into the concrete step before rolling off the porch and into the thick juniper bush adjacent to the home.

Henry didn't notice the red, white and blue hidden in the evergreen until a week later when he was mowing the lawn and saw the sleek metal eagle resting lifelessly on a thin branch.

Waiting for His Wife

"Where's my wife?" Joseph asked for the third time in five minutes.

"Dad, I already told you. She's not coming." The son held Joseph's brittle hand with a firm gentleness.

"Why..." he coughed twice "...not?"

The son looked at the grandson with pleading eyes.

The grandson shrugged and shook his head.

Three more coughs. The fecal stench overwhelmed everyone but Joseph. The son pushed the red button again. "Where's the goddamn nurse?" he shouted.

Three minutes passed. "Where's my wife?" Joseph asked again.

Joseph had been so handsome in his younger days. Even in his older days, he had been a fine specimen of man. His body had been strong and thick. His skin had been tan and smooth. His hair had been full. None of that was true anymore. The body was wasting away. At the current rate, he would be a skeleton in a week. The multiple myeloma, accompanied by the kidney failure, had been too much for any single human to overcome, no matter how strong that single human may have been, no matter how many torturous days he had fought in some war sixty years ago. He had given up. He had come here to die. All he wanted was his wife at his side.

"Dad..." the son began to explain before trailing off. There was no point. He would never understand that his wife had suffered from a stroke two nights ago and was now in a permanent coma at a different hospital until her death. She had been strong and faithful to the very end, spending countless hours beside his bedside, desperately trying everything to get him to eat, to get him to fight, to get him to live. Perhaps the stroke was her own way of giving up.

The son couldn't take the smell anymore. He stormed out of the room, leaving the grandson alone with the grandfather. In the hallway, he found a nurse drinking coffee. "How long does my father have to soak in his own shit before you come clean him up?"

The nurse swallowed her coffee. "Sir, we're short-staffed today. It's Labor Day weekend. We'll get to your father when we can."

"How's the coffee?" he asked smugly. "When you're finished with your pick-me-up, do you think that maybe you could come treat my father like a human so he can die a somewhat dignified death?"

The nurse sighed and slammed her coffee down on a countertop. She stormed off to find some help. The son returned to his father's room and found the boy staring silently at Joseph. The grandson's eyes were dry.

Joseph looked up with hopeful eyes. "Where's my wife?"

The son couldn't take it anymore either. "She's dying, Dad. She's in a coma and she's dying. She's never coming back. She's dying." Tears ran freely down his swollen red cheeks. Joseph stared blankly, ready to open his mouth and ask again, but something about the way his son looked at him made him close it. The son thought about apologizing, but there were too many things to be sorry for. When a nurse finally came in, the son hid the tears. The grandson still had not cried.

Joseph looked at the nurse and said, "Where's my wife?"

The nurse looked at the son and grandson, then approached Joseph. "Just try to relax, Mr. Venebal," she said as she lifted him and began the cleansing process.

"Where's my wife?" he muttered almost inaudibly, his face buried in the pillow as she cleaned the waste beneath him. The nurse didn't answer. The pillow didn't answer. No one answered. No matter how many times the words were said, no one could tell him. His brain had deteriorated beyond comprehension. All he could know at this point was that his wife was supposed to be there but wasn't. "Where's my wife?" he asked again when the nurse turned him back over.

"Close your eyes," she said. He did. She took his hand and cleared her throat. "I'm right here," she said to him. "I have to say goodbye now, though. I'll meet you in heaven."

Joseph smiled. The nurse squeezed his hand and left. The son cried. The grandson watched, unable to cry. The grandfather waited in the bed to die. The son and grandson waited for that as well.

Within a week, Joseph and his wife both passed. At the military burial, the horn playing "Taps" and the three-gun salute made the grandson cry. The thought of the husband and wife together in heaven free of sickness made the son smile.

Acknowledgements

There are many people to thank for making *Nagging Wives, Foolish Husbands* possible. This collection could not exist without the advice, help, and feedback from all the editors and fellow writers who perused these words. In particular, I'd like to thank Matthew Guerruckey of *Drunk Monkeys* for believing in so many of my wild stories. I'd also like to thank and praise Sarah McDaniel Dyer of *Old Timey Hedgehog*. Through her excellent editorial foresight and guidance, a story like "Laundry Day" actually works.

Of course, this collection also wouldn't work without the generosity and support of Julian Darius and Jeff Chon at *Martian Lit*.

A special thank you to everyone at Zoetrope's Flash Factory for supporting and encouraging my bizarre work. Several of these stories started there, and your comments shaped them into real pieces of fiction.

And the biggest thank you of all to my wife, for not rolling her eyes or nagging me about these stories. Without you, I'd probably just be a fool.

About the Author

Nathaniel Tower lives in the Twin Cities area with his wife and daughter. After teaching high school English for nine years, he decided to start a new career in writing / publishing / editing. His fiction has appeared in over two hundred online and print journals. In 2011, MuseItUp Publishing released his first novel, *A Reason to Kill*, followed a year later by his first novella, *Hallways and Handguns*. Nathaniel is the founding and managing editor of *Bartleby Snopes Literary Magazine and Press*. When he's not doing writerly things, he likes to joggle (juggle and run simultaneously). He is the former world record holder for running a mile backwards while juggling. He is working on getting his record back. Find out more about Nathaniel at nathanieltower.wordpress.com.